MAGIC STREET BOOGIE

MAGIC STREET BOOGIE

SCIONS OF MAGIC™ BOOK ONE

TR CAMERON

MICHAEL ANDERLE

This book is a work of fiction. All of the characters, organizations, and events portrayed in this novel are either products of the author's imagination or are used fictitiously. Sometimes both.

Cover Art by Jake @ J Caleb Design
http://jcalebdesign.com / jcalebdesign@gmail.com

A Michael Anderle Production

LMBPN Publishing
PMB 196, 2540 South Maryland Pkwy
Las Vegas, NV 89109

First US edition, November, 2019
Version 1.02, February 2020
ebook ISBN: 978-1-64202-567-5
Print: 978-1-64202-568-2

Beta Team
Larry Omans, Nicole Emens, Kelly O'Donnell, John Ashmore

Thanks to the JIT Readers

Dave Hicks
Jeff Eaton
Micky Cocker
Deb Mader
Paul Westman

If I've missed anyone, please let me know!

Editor
Skyhunter Editing Team

DEDICATIONS

Dedication: For those who seek wonder around every corner and in each turning page. And, as always, for Dylan.

— *TR Cameron*

To Family, Friends and
Those Who Love
To Read.
May We All Enjoy Grace
To Live The Life We Are
Called.

— *Michael*

CHAPTER ONE

The dwarf behind the bar yelled, "Hey, idiots. Knock it off."

Cali Leblanc slapped the groping hands of the frat boy foursome away as she made her way to the long divider of polished wood that separated the owner from his patrons. She set the tray down a little harder than intended and shook her head at Zeb. "Tourists, right?"

The Drunken Dragons Tavern was a locals bar. More than that, it provided a haven where the city's magical beings could congregate, more often than not in peaceful coexistence. It lay on the outskirts of the French Quarter, which meant most of the out-of-towners visiting New Orleans for vacation, business, or the intensive debauchery of Mardi Gras never knew it existed. The wooden placard hung outside over the entrance featured a red dragon clinking beer steins with a blue one, both recently repainted. Their cheap crystal eyes flashed when the sun caught them.

She raised an eyebrow as she resumed their long-standing argument. "You know it's the damn gems in the sign that attract them, right? You can see the things from blocks away."

Zeb patted the impressive dark thatch of hair that lay against his chest and shook his head. His smile was mostly lost in the beard and mustache that covered his face, but the crinkles around his stunning blue eyes suggested he still enjoyed the game as much as she did. "Their money spends. As long as they don't cause trouble with the regulars or the staff, they're welcome."

As she was the only person at the moment who qualified as staff, his meaning was apparent. His bellows across the single main room took care of most issues before they started, and his gaze always seemed to be on her when someone tried to interfere with her work. *I only wish he'd give the cute ones a little more time before he scares them away.* Seven and a half months before, after the worst day of her life, the dwarf had appointed himself her de facto guardian and had proven both his aptitude and his over-enthusiasm for the role ever since.

She removed and re-secured the elastic that restrained her curly red hair and wiped her forehead. Even with the air conditioner doing its best, October in the south was an oven and work always made her feel half-cooked. Unlike some drinking places around town, The Drunken Dragons didn't go in for skimpy outfits to entice tourists. Her standard work uniform of black jeans, matching boots, and a white button-down with a tank beneath was as neutral as could be. But, unfortunately, it did little to help her to keep her cool.

As if he could read her mind—and who knew, maybe he

could—Zeb handed her a glass of iced water that she guzzled. She knew very little about his magic, and on the rare occasions when she'd tried to pry for more, he'd deflected her questions smoothly. Really, she was only positive about three things where the dwarf was concerned. First, he was originally from Oriceran, the magical planet that crossed over with Earth more each day. Second, he watched over her with the intensity of a hawk tracking a limping rabbit. And finally, he believed in shutting down small problems before they became big ones, usually with a sharp tongue and loud voice.

Cali lowered her head. "Yeah, but some people aren't worth the trouble their money buys." The design of the establishment reflected his desire to keep an eye on his patrons. Long wooden tables ran the length of the room, butted up against one another to form three separate rows with benches and chairs on both sides. On a busy night, elves would rub elbows with gnomes, and the occasional giant Kilomea would spread into space allocated for four.

No species was prohibited, and the only rule was that they take any conflicts outside the walls. The dwarf's glower was sufficient threat to forestall most potential inappropriate behavior, but a wicked-looking double-bladed battle ax hung behind the bar to back it up. She'd never seen it leave its position.

Zeb pulled a pipe from beneath the counter and took several puffs before he stowed it again. Sweet tobacco smoke filled the air between them. Even when he wasn't actively smoking, his clothes smelled of the stuff so much that she now associated it with him. Technically, the tavern was smoke-free, so he kept his vice hidden most of the time. "They're simply young fools. Maybe get them to eat something, though." A crash sounded from the direction of the foursome, and she swiveled her head to see that two of them stood with fists raised. "Okay, they're young, stupid, fools. Go break it up."

She dodged and wove between the revelers on her way to the men. Even though the rest of the patrons didn't seem to care about the impending battle, it was still crowded enough on this Friday night to make movement a challenge. Both chuckleheads were dressed alike in t-shirts with beer logos on them, jean shorts, and slip-on shoes. *If you're going to be a stereotype, why that stereotype?*

When she reached them, they were exchanging taunts while each tried to muster the nerve to start something and, when they failed, attempted to goad their opponent into doing so. She slid smoothly into the gap between them and pushed them apart with a hand on each of their chests.

"Listen, guys, I'm not sure what has you ticked off, but this isn't the place. If you want to fight, take it outside. Otherwise, you might disturb the patrons, and these aren't the type of folks you want to get upset at you." They looked first at her, then at the room around them, and finally at each other.

She thought she had them convinced, but the taste of black licorice washed over her tongue as her magic read the men through her touch. It was stronger from her right, and that man sneered predictably and drew his arm back for a punch. She sighed before she ducked under it, caught his wrist, and wrenched it down with a twist. He howled and dropped to a knee. She raised her other hand to point at his foe. "Don't even think about it." He backed away, his palms raised.

From the direction of the bar came a gruff, "Pay up and begone, you four," and she nodded.

"You heard the man. I'll release your friend here once you all are outside." He attempted to rise, and she twisted his wrist against the bone, which drew a yelp. She scowled down at him. "Behave, you, or I'll let the boss take care of you. Trust me, yours wouldn't be the first blood he's washed off that ax." He paled, and she looked up in time to see Zeb smother a smile. Finally, the others were gone and she freed her captive. He rubbed his arm as he rose, and she kept her weight equally balanced in case he decided to try something she'd need to deal with. The smarter part of his brain won out, and he flipped her off and made his way to the exit.

She collected their cups to the sound of the room's low laughter as the door slammed closed behind them. A Dark Elf she particularly liked raised a fist, and she bumped it with a smile. She set the glasses on the bar and the dwarf moved over to collect them for washing. He offered her a grin. "Well done. You have a way with idiots."

A chuckle escaped her. "You realize you totally set yourself up, right?"

He nodded. "But you're far too wise to take advantage."

Cali leaned both elbows on the polished wood and invoked another of their frequent discussion topics. "You know, aren't you supposed to be the rage-driven warrior? Why do I fight your battles for you?"

Like always, he grinned and tapped his temple. "Brains over brawn. I'm smart enough to have you do it for me."

His eyes flicked over her shoulder, and he shook his head with a sigh "Jarten ran without paying. Again. Stop him but don't hurt him. Much."

She spun and dashed to the door. *It's not Friday night if I don't have to chase some idiot over the price of a drink or two.*

Her quarry was one of the many people of Atlantean descent who populated the Big Easy. The legendary undersea city had really existed like the legends said, but its population was originally from Oriceran. Atlantis had been destroyed long before, but the bloodline lived on, strong enough to be seen easily in some but weak enough to be invisible in others. In Jarten, it was weak.

Her own half-Atlantean lineage was most visible in her hair, which was thick, curly, and frequently downright annoying.

His magical ancestry didn't make the man she pursued any faster than normal. His lead dwindled rapidly as he pounded along the street. He turned into an alley, and his head swiveled left and right, up and down, as he sought options. Fortunately for her, these houses were similar to many in the town and protected by high walls topped with sharp rocks, broken glass, or pointed iron spikes. When she'd closed the gap to six feet, she yelled, "Jar, knock it off, you idiot. It's not like you won't be back in a week."

He flashed out of sight ahead, and she skidded to a stop as she rounded the corner and discovered three other people standing with him. They all looked to be close to the age when they'd graduate college if they actually attended. Two were male and of a body type similar to Jarten's, which meant tall and thin. The woman was her height, which was to say neither tall nor short but had at least twenty pounds on her, all of it muscle. Cali nodded. "Folks. See if you can get chucklehead there to pay the tab he owes at the tavern."

The others stepped in front of her quarry and the obvious defensive action drew a sigh from her. The tallest of the group raised his head and looked down his sharp nose. His Atlantean blood was obvious in his thick hair, which was gathered into ratty dreadlocks. He spoke with an unexpectedly low, gravelly voice. "How about you cover this one for him? And, if you're feeling kind, you could cough up a few bucks for us, too."

She would have imagined Jarten would be the runt of the litter, but the third man added a postscript in a weaseling tone. "Yeah, I could use a few bucks." Cali met the eyes of the group's lone female, who shook her head in shared disappointment at the other gender but made no move to step away from her friends. No Atlantean blood was obvious in her, but it seemed almost a certainty that it was there. She'd heard rumors that Jarten was running with a group who drew lines based on ethnicity but hadn't realized it was a magical one. Her guess had been Cajun, given his accent. *I guess not.*

Cali neither retreated nor showed concern. "Here's the thing. My boss sent me out to bring back what Jar owes. I don't care if it comes from him or if y'all take up a collection to support the stupidest among you, but I'll leave here with it or with him. Come on, we're talking ten bucks." It was really six, but she decided she deserved something for running in the heat.

The man with the voice broke into a grin. "You may want to rethink that. There are four of us. And while you may think your karate is fancy, we have our own talents as well."

"Him or the money." She shrugged. "Now would be good."

Their leader gestured, and the least among them charged, holding something in his hand. She identified it as a tree branch, still with twigs attached, and he scratched a line of red onto his face when he brought it toward her in a wild swing. Even though they'd broken the seal and implied they had magic, she wasn't ready to reveal hers unless it became necessary. Her father's voice, kindly and encouraging, had reminded her often to "Always keep your hole card hidden."

She skipped inside the arc of the wood and delivered a sharp punch that channeled the power of her movement into his solar plexus. He gasped and dropped out of the fight for the moment. She looked from his prone form back to her foes' spokesperson. "So, can we call this done?"

He peered over his shoulder at the woman, and she stalked forward. Her thick legs showed rippling muscles below her cutoff jeans, and the tank top she wore bared powerful arms. Cali shook her head. *I could look like that if I spent more time in the gym. Or any time in the gym.*

Her opponent led with a wrestling technique, faked a bear hug, and tried to power past to get behind her. Cali set her feet and let it happen. Before the other woman could lock an arm around her neck, however, she dropped into a crouch and pistoned her elbow up and back while she twisted her core with the strike. This adversary, too, succumbed to the solar plexus blow, but it required a quick foot sweep to bring her to the ground. She moved away from the downed figures and circled left to ensure a clear space to act.

The leader waved at Jarten, who shook his head. The man slapped him on the side of the head, but the object of her search didn't comply. Finally, the bigger man growled, "Okay, girl, let's do this."

She snapped, "Don't call me girl," as he raised his arms. She performed a reasonably proficient cartwheel to her left as the space between them filled with wavering light and the fence behind her shattered. Thankfully, she'd guessed he'd go for the home run right off the bat, and the best defense was to not be in the way of it. Her martial arts training was all about avoiding blows rather than standing tall in front of them. She waved her hand, imagined herself running away, and summoned an illusion to make it look real while another appeared to mask her lack of actual movement.

As he spun to launch an attack at the visible false-Cali, she stepped into his blind spot and hooked his outstretched arm. After a thrust of her hip and twist of her body, he launched over her to land hard on the pavement. She turned in case Jarten planned to use her distraction to deliver a sucker punch, but instead, he used it to run. With a sigh at the need to expend more magic, she directed a thin force beam at his feet. He squealed as he tripped and fell.

She yanked his wallet from his back pocket and pulled

out the ten-dollar bill he had inside. "You really are an idiot, you know that? From now on, you pay in advance. Your friends too."

The others seemed to make some effort at recovery so she jogged away before they could gather the confidence to try her again. Jarten's words reached her from a distance but were clear nonetheless. "You'll be sorry you messed with us. Count on it."

"I'm already sorry," she retorted over her shoulder. *If they're smart, they'll leave it alone. If not...well, guess I'll deal with that problem when it arrives.* With a start, she realized that Zeb had been on his own in the bar for almost ten minutes and increased her speed. If anyone else decided to cause trouble, she'd need to be there to intercept it. She had never seen and had no desire to know what her boss was like when he was truly angry.

CHAPTER TWO

Tanyith cowered in his bare cell as the storm raged on the opposite side of the dark stone wall. The other captives housed within Trevilsom Prison doubtless perceived the cacophony as yet another threat added to the madness-invoking properties of the island that was home to the structure. To him, it was a balm, a reminder of who he was.

And it came barely in time. He'd thought that this would be the one that broke him. The stretch of what others in his old life would describe as "decent weather" provided him with no surcease from the whispers that muddled what was real and what was imaginary. Those murmurings would eventually shatter his ability to discern the difference between the two and condemn him to madness eternal.

But the storm had come, the tempest as soothing as the Atlantean portion of his nature, which had become more and more ascendant as the months passed and everything less stubborn was consumed by the prison. To the best of his knowledge, he had survived with his sanity intact for longer than any prisoner before him. He'd asked the silent sentinels who oversaw the facility, but they refused to respond. Even if they had, he wouldn't have been able to trust their words or truly know whether they really had replied or if it was merely his imagination.

He focused on the sounds of the crashing waves, timed the thunder to the flashes of light that stabbed through his small window, inhaled the scent of the rain, and surrendered his mind to those known things as a way to keep the unknown and untrustworthy away.

The storm was long and furious, and as time was meaningless in Trevilsom, he had no idea how much had passed when other strange sounds emerged through the tumultuous sound of the weather. A rhythmic pounding sounded like metal on stone, almost buried under the crash of the waves on the jagged rocks that marked the perimeter between land and water. This was followed by a lighter version of the same sound and finally, a scrabbling that made him think a small animal was scaling the wall outside his cell.

Such a thing was impossible, of course. Animals were not immune to the madness, and the ones that stumbled onto the island didn't live long enough to play any role other than a meal for the prisoners. Tanyith shrieked and crabbed away from the window when a dark face appeared. He hadn't heard a voice other than the whispers and the other inmates' screams for so long that when it spoke, he almost couldn't comprehend the language. The eye-roll was instantly understandable as she—it sounded like a she—spoke again. "Are you Tanyith?"

He nodded, then forced the words from his throat. "Yes. Tanyith. Yes. How? Who?"

She shook her head, clearly exasperated. "Call me Nylotte. The rest can wait. And don't move."

Her face disappeared from the window, and it required all his restraint not to rush over to ensure she'd been real. Lightning flashed and he counted for the thunder. When it sounded, the outer wall cracked and a portion fell away to reveal a hole to the outside about three feet up. He delayed, his brain slow to process, and she hissed in irritation. "Now, Tanyith. There's no time."

The prisoner ran forward and pushed through the opening, his formerly muscular body slender enough to fit easily. Her strong arms helped him to climb free and stand, and she steadied him with one hand while she pressed a vial into his palm with the other. "My boat is destroyed and the island defeats my ability to portal. I can't get us out of here. You have to do it."

He looked down idly and prepared to tell her that the trip had been in vain and that his power had abandoned him. The sight of the bright blue liquid coursing in the clear container, glowing with energy of its own, almost killed him with desire. He yanked the top off, drank it quickly, and threw the bottle aside as magical energy swept through him. Tanyith spun, grasped the Dark Elf, and launched himself over the rocks in a powerful jump that carried them both into the lake ahead of the late-reacting guards' crossbow bolts.

The sensation of being submerged was everything. Water had always been his solace, and it had been denied him during his time behind the prison bars. A translucent magical cocoon surrounded them to ensure they'd have air. As much as he wanted to feel the liquid on his skin, he'd been separated from his power for so long that he didn't trust his ability to make such minute adjustments to the spell. She whispered, "Northeast," and his senses reached out to chart the currents and the magnetic fields that influenced them. He altered course to the correct direction and applied a special version of force magic that worked most effectively in water to speed their progress.

In minutes, she climbed out of the lake while he lay on his back with only his nose above the surface, luxuriating in the opportunity to simply float. After what seemed like only an instant, she called out, "Tanyith, we're not out of danger yet. We have to keep moving." He left the water reluctantly and she handed him a long cloak and a belt, which made him realize his nakedness for the first time in an age. He shrugged into them with a lopsided grin.

"Prison life didn't suit me all that well."

She laughed. "It's amazing you were able to survive for so long."

He frowned. "I…lost track of time." There was no point in trying to explain how the prison had broken parts of him or how it had almost broken all of him. *The sooner I start putting it in the past, the better.*

A man spoke and surprised him. He'd seen him before but forgotten him almost as quickly, his skittering attention making it difficult to keep thoughts in his head. "You've been in there for thirteen months. I was approached a month ago, and Nylotte joined the team two weeks ago. It took most of that time to work out a plan that wouldn't get us all killed. The prison's defenses are formidable. Only importing a certain kind of explosive from Earth made it possible."

Tanyith chuckled darkly. "If there's one thing my home planet is good at, it's creating ways to hurt people." He frowned. "And if there's a second thing, it's a penchant for betrayal."

The man tapped the patch he wore over his eye. "I am well aware of the risks that come with getting involved with your planet. I am, by the way, Chadrousse."

Nylotte, who had gathered packs resting on the ground nearby, pushed one into his hands. "And we all have to move. Now. The guards might not be able to leave the island easily but that doesn't mean they lack allies who can come in pursuit. We have miles to walk before it will be safe to portal, so we'd best get to it."

He held up well for the initial half-hour of the trek through the sparse forest, trading his dwindling magic for muscle fuel, but reached a point where his body succumbed and he sank to the ground in a small clearing. Nylotte and Chadrousse agreed to a halt, and she handed him actual food, the first non-disgusting fare he'd had in over a year. He nibbled carefully around the edges of the fruit and nut rectangle and sipped from the canteen she provided.

Chadrousse complained, "Certainly we're far enough now."

The Drow shook her head. "There's a reason Trevilsom is so feared. I'm not sure how far its influence spreads or at what range it can detect and possibly intercept magic. We need more distance." She handed him one of the bars, and he took it with another grumble. She turned to the escapee and kept her smile hidden from the other man. "He's crabby—more of a delegator than a doer if you know what I mean. But this task required both of us. We needed a backup in case I didn't survive the break-in."

He sighed away a tiny sliver of the collected stress of his imprisonment. *It'll take a long time to get over this experience.* His brain seemed to click better, though, and a question occurred to him. "Why did you do this? What do I owe you? Or him?"

The Dark Elf lowered herself to the ground beside her pack and rifled through it. "I did it because Chadrousse made it a condition in exchange for some knowledge I needed. That's what he does. He trades information for favors." She made a noise of victory and pulled another vial out of the satchel, this one filled with a dusky red liquid that looked somehow viscous. "Why did he do it? I guess because he received something valuable for being the broker in the deal. I don't think he anticipated having to jeopardize his own skin in person, though."

She extended the vial, and he leaned forward to take it. "Healing?"

"Yes. I didn't have access to any Atlanteans to test it on, so its potency will be low. I couldn't risk an adverse effect, so I merely made it sustaining rather than fully rejuvenating."

Tanyith chuckled. "You're not from New Orleans, then. We're all over the place down there." He twisted the top from the container and took a sip, then smiled as a taste of honey spread over his tongue and brought strength and warmth along with it. His smile of thanks earned a brief nod. He gave her time to offer information about herself, but she remained silent and stared at him like she was judging him. "What?"

"I'm waiting for the story."

"What story?"

She raised an eyebrow. "What you did to get locked up in Trevilsom, of course. What kind of person have we set free?"

He laughed darkly. "You don't know?"

"No." She turned to the other man. "Rousse, any idea what he did to get planted on the island?"

Her co-conspirator swiveled his head from where he stood in profile and stared at the surrounding land like he could see trouble coming if he only looked hard enough. "It didn't come up. They were willing to give me what I wanted and he was the price. Why would I care?"

Nylotte shrugged as she faced him again. "So, what's the deal?"

"You won't believe it."

She laughed. "After the last year, I'm prepared to believe one hell of a lot."

Tanyith spread his hands to the side. "I didn't break the law at all. What I did do was tick off the wrong person."

Her head tilted. "Who?"

He shook his head with a sad chuckle. "Yeah, that's the question, isn't it? I've tried to think of the answer for a little over thirteen months. All I'm sure of is that they're connected to a certain group of Atlanteans in NOLA. And, when I get back, I'll find out and have a very serious conversation with whoever was behind this." He tilted the rest of the vial into his mouth, and the flow of health felt like fate promising him that his vengeance was guaranteed.

The woman blew a breath out. "Fantastic. Exactly what I need in my life, another person with hidden enemies. I'm not sure what supreme being I annoyed, but at this point, I'd be willing to make a sweetheart of a deal to set it right." She flowed to her feet and lifted the pack to shrug it onto her shoulders. When she pointed at him and at the one nearest him, he rose in response. The last one, she grabbed and gestured at her partner. "Let's go, Chadrousse. Tanyith needs to get back to his hometown. Apparently, there are secrets to be discovered. You haven't actually collected them all."

The other man sauntered over, stylish and clean in a way that neither of his companions could currently achieve. He made a distasteful face as he submitted to her efforts to put the pack on his back, then smiled. "You know, my new friend, if you discover you need information, I have access to almost any knowledge you could desire to possess."

From behind him came a deep sigh, followed by the Drow's wry voice. "Hopefully, he'll be smarter than that. Learn from my lesson, Tanyith. Trading favors is nothing but trouble."

CHAPTER THREE

Cali yawned as she ran the dry mop over the large mat that filled the center of the Aikido dojo. She'd managed six hours of sleep, which was about her average, before her phone woke her with the jangly cover of "Thunderstruck" by Steve'n'Seagulls. After sleeping through every alarm or song she'd tried, her last option was to buy an app that randomized her alarms with selections from a list of high-intensity songs one of her friends curated for her. *And we'll have a conversation about including banjo in my wake-up music as soon as I see him.*

The dojo opened at ten, and she arrived four days a week by eight-thirty to get things ready. For the first six months, Sensei Ikehara Goro had been present each morning. After she'd proven herself, he had entrusted her with a key and the responsibility to prepare the training space. It was a fair trade—free instruction whenever she could fit a class into her schedule in exchange for mindless cleaning and straightening. In truth, she enjoyed the alone time and reveled in the silence that was the antithesis of her main job.

It gave her an opportunity to think and today, she thought about Jarten and his friends and wondered when the other shoe from that encounter would drop. While she'd been careful not to overly damage anyone, wounded pride might push them to a rematch. She shrugged as she stored the mop and went up front to clean the windows. *You can't control what they do, only what you do.* Another of her father's favorite sayings, and she missed him more with each one that surfaced in her memory.

Ikehara entered and made a point of reviewing her work, as he always did. At first, it had been real, she was sure. Now, she was ninety percent positive that it was only for show but that didn't stop her from taking the task seriously. The admonition, "Do your best or don't bother doing it at all," came from her mother, who she missed as much as her other parent. She doubted she'd ever get past the pain of their deaths.

"Caliste," he said sharply and she cringed. The only time people tended to use the long form of her name was when she was in trouble.

"Yes, Sensei?"

"You have done an excellent job, as always. How are your studies?"

She shrugged. "Progressing, but slowly."

He nodded. His facial structure and dark eyes displayed his Japanese heritage, and both his dark crewcut and his thin shadow of beard and mustache showed his attention to martial detail, denying an enemy something to latch onto. His accent was notable even though he'd been in

New Orleans for most of his fifty years, and she loved the sound of it. "The important part is staying on the path. One day, you will be a fine—what is it, criminal investigator?"

"Yes, Sensei." *One day a long long way from this one at the rate of six courses a year, that is.* She lacked time, funds, and focus to do more than that. Losing her parents had dashed the hopes she'd had for a typical college experience and for a normal life. Now, she worked at the tavern, lived alone in a small room in a historic boarding house, did homework for her online classes at the public library, and traded cleaning for learning at the dojo. In the hours that remained, she hung out at Jackson Square, busking with her friends. She often thought it suited her better than a traditional path might have.

The sensei smiled broadly. "Very good. Now, go prepare for class." He insisted she take ten minutes to meditate and clear her thoughts, and it took another ten to dress in the aikido uniform. Those twenty minutes allowed her to change her headspace from worker to learner. It also improved her ability to block off parts of her mind at need. Sometimes, when a customer was being particularly annoying at the tavern, that skill was the only thing that saved the offender from eating a force bolt.

She used several items as touchstones while meditating. Wide silver rings engraved with ornate designs encircled each thumb. She pressed her hands together and touched the metal bands to the brass and silver disc that hung from a matching chain. It was as thick as a locket but had no seams or opening mechanism. Her parents had given the jewelry to her a year before their deaths, instructing her to never take them off. At the time, she'd obeyed because they were the authority in her life. Now, she continued in honor of them.

One thing she packed away into a corner of her mind was her intention-reading ability. While it would be potentially valuable in a real fight, it would be a crutch in her training. No one was aware that she could do it, not even Zeb. The power had developed after her parents were gone and she didn't feel comfortable discussing it with anyone. It was personal to her in a way that her other magics, which she knew were shared by many others of Oriceran descent, weren't.

When the arrival of her classmates banished her solitude, she emerged and began her stretching. Her chosen position was in the corner of the room farthest from the changing areas and the entrance. She worked through poses and mimed throws until the mat filled and her teacher clapped to signal the start of class. The students quickly arranged themselves, and Ikehara-Sensei took his place facing the front row. He wore a white top, black belt, and the split-legged hakama that was the telltale of an Aikido master. First, he led the white-uniformed and belted men and women through the warmups and stances, then into tumbling and break-falls.

Cali wasn't much of an acrobat but she was agile, and her diligent practice showed as she landed cleanly and rolled easily into the next position. She was partnered with a woman who was a little shorter than her and looked to be about ten years older. Sweat glistened on her forehead and she breathed heavily. If they'd been grappling opponents, she would have worked to tire her, stayed on the move rather than going for the quick victory, and trusted that her own endurance would win out. Together, they practiced throws and joint locks under the watchful eyes of the teacher, who interrupted them several times to adjust and advise.

The end of the class varied each day. They would finish sometimes grappling, sometimes focusing on the kicks and punches that were not technically Aikido but Ikehara valued anyway, and sometimes, like today, weapons instruction. Again, her sensei bucked tradition by including not only the traditional bokken, jo, and tanto, but escrima sticks as well. He claimed dual-wielding the weapon added useful pathways in the mind, different from the directness of the sword and knife and the flourish of the staff. The room was filled with swishes, slaps, and cracks as they fought one another at slow speed, training the muscles to remember the movements.

By the time it was over, Cali was energized. Some students seemed tired and happy as they left. Others were unmoved, but she was always lit up by the sessions. She changed quickly and offered a rigid, deep bow to her instructor as she departed. Ikehara returned a nod of acknowledgment before he shifted his attention to a potential student who had wandered in to watch the end of class.

It was a couple of miles to Jackson Square. She kept her mind light and watched people as she passed them. Residents out for walks gave way to hungover tourists who squinted against the pain of the bright sunlight. The streets still smelled of the bleach used to clean them overnight as the heat of the day baked away whatever puddles of liquid had resisted its earlier efforts. She wove through the quarter, avoiding the most touristy areas in favor of the ones she knew best. Finally, she arrived at the square and headed to the most profitable corner, the one nearest Cafe du Monde.

The object of her scanning gaze located her before she found him and his shout covered the distance between them. "Cal, s'up?"

She turned toward the sound and her gaze settled on her closest comrade, Dasante Parks. He waved to catch her attention and she threaded through the buskers working the street—the ever-present painted statue people, a mime, a thin man dressed in a Snow White costume but with a face made skeletal by stage makeup, and a big woman who belted the blues out on a saxophone. Finally, she reached him and stepped behind his battered folding magician's table.

"Same old, Dee." They performed an intricate handshake involving slaps and fist bumps that brought grins to both their faces. He wore a black dress shirt only a few shades darker than his skin, the sleeves rolled up as part of his act. She flicked imaginary lint from his shoulder with a grin. "You're a mess." He wasn't any kind of a mess, of course, and the way his long straightened inky hair fell over half his face was decidedly cute.

He laughed. "Well, all right, then. What's the plan for today, girl?"

She shrugged. "I thought some frozen fighting if someone's around." One of her favorite performances to give was pretending to battle in slow motion. Passersby seemed to like it, often stopped to watch, and less often dropped a dollar or two in the backpack she put out for that purpose. She had other personas too, but they required more effort and didn't fit well into the time between the dojo and the tavern.

He grinned. "Bark for me?"

"Sure. Happy to." There was no need to ask about the financial arrangements because she only worked with those willing to go fifty-fifty. She scrabbled in her back-pack, retrieved an elastic, and bound her hair behind her. The black jeans and t-shirt were adequate, so all she needed was a touch of makeup. She reddened her lips and darkened her eyes to make them easier to see from a distance and took a position in front of the table near the street.

Working the streets as a performer combined with shouting down idiots in the tavern had built her voice into a far stronger tool than anyone would expect, and she put it to use. "Magic, prestidigitation, sleight of hand. See the amazing Dasante as he performs close-up feats that will blow your mind. Find the cup with the ball in it and win a reward." She'd picked flowers along her walk that morning because it was always good to have something to say thank you with. "You, sir—surely you can beat him." She pointed at a college-age man with all the signs of a tourist, including the doting woman on his arm.

He tried to wave her off, but she shook her head. "Come on, now, impress your girlfriend. You have nothing to lose." They looked at each other and laughed, then came over to watch. Dasante let the man win the first two rounds to earn a flower for each of them, then put his skill into the next two, hiding it beyond the man's ability to guess. A few more people had stopped to watch the act, and she grinned as he finished with one of his best simple tricks—making the white ball vanish but replacing it with red balls under all three cups. There was applause and a brief shower of bills and coins landed in the upended top hat resting on the ground in front of his table.

They worked the crowd for a couple of hours, trading entertainment for tips. By the time the lunchtime population began to fade, she was ready to call it a day and head to the tavern for a pre-shift meal and a nap in the back of the kitchen. As she picked her backpack up, Dasante spoke in a low tone. "Don't look now, but there's someone who's watched us for the last twenty minutes or so. You'll want to keep an eye out for him. Across the street, two o'clock."

She didn't react to his words, only shrugged the bag on and turned to give him a parting handshake. Long before, she had mastered the trick of looking intently without appearing to do so, and she immediately saw the man in question. He was dark-skinned and had black hair in braids falling around his face and was clad in a ratty t-shirt and baggy jeans. She finished the goodbye and thanked her friend for the information. When she started to move, the watcher did too but immediately, he melted into the crowd and out of sight.

I'm not sure why an Atlantean is surveilling me, but I'll damned sure find out. The loss of her nap and the growling in her stomach were forgotten as she dashed across the street in pursuit.

CHAPTER FOUR

Her senses on alert, Cali approached the alley warily and stuck her head quickly around the corner to discover her quarry was no longer in sight. A bird cawed at her from overhead and she wished momentarily that she could question it, but that wasn't part of her magic arsenal either. She pulled her hair free from the elastic and rolled her t-shirt up to show a little skin as a hasty disguise. With a promise that she'd start carrying something better or improve her illusion skills, she pounded down the narrow corridor after the man.

She skidded to a halt and eased her head around the corner as the passage ended, which drew confused looks from several people walking past. The sidewalk traffic was one of the things she loved about the town and provided so many different individuals to look at. But for a foot pursuit, it was a decided negative. Fortunately, her quarry was tall enough that his braids were visible, like a beacon drawing her eyes directly to it. She plunged into the flow of pedestrians, kept him in sight, and snaked closer whenever the current permitted it.

He stopped at a corner and looked down, and as she drew closer, the person on the ground came into view. He held a sign asking for money for beer. *Points for honesty, anyway.* His skin was lighter than the braided man's but far darker than her own. Their body language made them seem more like acquaintances than friends, but it was enough that she didn't want to pass and let him see her.

Another alley provided the solution. She darted inside and clambered up onto a closed-top dumpster, vaulted, and caught the iron poles of the balcony above it. With more grace than awkwardness, she climbed over the railing, landed on the narrow surface, and ran up the stairs to the roof. The asphalt covering was sticky and it pulled at her boots with a sucking sound as she ran to peer over the edge. She frowned as the braided man dodged through traffic to the other side of the road and entered one of the many small shops that lined both sides of the street.

The bright daylight meant she couldn't use her magic. Under cover of darkness, she would have launched from the roof and relied on her force power to slow her fall. Instead, she scrambled back to the alley and to the exit at the end opposite from where she'd entered and walked slowly past the door he'd gone through. The view through the glass revealed a store filled with clothes, a decent looking selection based on a quick glance as she went past. Too many of the shops near the quarter focused on the tourist trade, and aside from her Saints jersey, she had little interest in the cheap New Orleans branded merchandise they peddled.

She didn't dare go in as it wasn't big enough to offer her any cover. A coffee shop was conveniently located a few doors down, however, so she slipped inside and took a seat at the window, ordered a cafe au lait, and drifted her gaze between her phone and the doorway. A momentary blank screen reflected her face to remind her that she still wore the barker makeup. She pulled out a wipe and cleaned it off, irritated that she hadn't thought of it already. *James Bond, I'm not.*

Her coffee arrived and she paid with cash so she could leave when she needed to. Slow sips savored the chicory brew, another of her favorite things about New Orleans. Finally, an eternal seven minutes after she'd finished, her quarry emerged with a bag over his shoulder. She looked down and away as he passed her window, merely a random person obsessed with her phone.

Cali stepped out and located him easily as he moved toward the street that marked the boundary of the French Quarter. She followed him across it and past the casino, thankful that he hadn't gone inside where it would be far harder to tail him. He entered a small restaurant and she groaned. *Will the jerk simply walk around doing nothing all day?* She didn't dare get close enough for him to see her again, so she sat on the sidewalk and tried to look tired and inconspicuous.

He was back ten minutes later, eating something out of a tin foil wrap. Two more people were with him and from behind, they looked similar—dark skin, dark hair, and thinner, shorter braids. They walked like friends who tried to be tough with a rolling stride that suggested hidden weapons under their long sports jerseys. The man she'd pursued was imposing without the posturing. Something about him conveyed the certainty that he wasn't someone who would react well to being followed.

Pedestrians thinned out as they continued. She began to despair that she would have to give up the chase when they stopped at a large building and knocked on the door. It opened almost instantly, and after a short conversational delay, they entered. She waited in case someone inside was watching for a tail, then walked slowly toward it. A mural on the front proclaimed that it was The Shark Nightclub. The only other notable feature on its facade was the bright red door that had swallowed the men.

She sauntered into the narrow alley that bordered the club and the building beside it. The passage was barely wide enough to accommodate two people walking together and was devoid of anything interesting. This wall of the club was equally featureless except for a side door, also bright red but without a handle. She peered around the back and discovered another entrance and a fenced-in area containing dumpsters. Her phone buzzed as she was about to climb the fence and try to reach the roof.

Cali yanked it out of her back pocket to find a message from Zeb telling her to get to the bar early because some important magical person was coming in with a group of other important magical people. She shrugged the back-pack higher on her shoulders and walked into the alley. Fortunately, she knew the basement of the tavern well and it was a simple matter to open a portal between that and her current location. A silver line sparkled in a circle as she drew it in the air with her index finger, then filled from the outside with a wavering image of the other location. She stepped through and collapsed the rift behind her.

Tanyith watched from the roof of a nearby building as the redhead made her magical exit. It had been a surprise to see her following one of the members of the Atlantean gang, and he was reasonably sure they hadn't noticed her. *Interesting. I wonder what she's up to? No matter. As long as she stays out of my way.*

CHAPTER FIVE

Tanyith's return to New Orleans had been shocking on several levels. First, the transition from prison into society was jarring. Loud noises made him flinch, and there were far too many of them, from friendly greetings to threatening bellows, the cheerful chime of the trolley bell, or the angry honks of frustrated drivers.

Second, many of the foundational truths of his previous life no longer existed. He'd had friends but could find none of them. The house he had lived in with several other like-minded individuals had burned down, to judge from the stray scorched lumber chips that still lay in the empty lot. Worst of all, his mentor and best friend Karam had vanished, his home sold to a human family. The neighborhood had felt wrong from his first step into it. The lack of Atlantean gang tags or street sentinels was an instant clue that something important had occurred. *Territory changed hands while I was away, which makes most of my hard-earned street knowledge nothing more than an old man's ramblings of the past.*

At twenty-seven, Tanyith was hardly old, but his time in Trevilsom had aged him in body and mind. As far as he knew, there was no one to ask about how long it would take to recover or if it was even possible to repair the damage. Despite that, his gratitude for being away from that horrible place could still stop him in his tracks for fear it was an illusion or that he was dreaming if he focused on it too hard.

After the strange would-be-spy woman had left, he had remained on the roof across from the nightclub for the rest of the afternoon and into the evening. He used small, subtle magics that were unlikely to be detected to convince the breeze to keep him cool and to veil himself from sight with the help of the wavering heat rising from the black surface beneath his boots. The dirty blue jeans and too-tight t-shirt stolen from a second-hand store were dark enough to not stand out in the shadow of the chimney at his back.

The club was a quandary. Fourteen months before, it had been one of the most popular nightspots for Atlanteans in the Crescent City. He'd been inside any number of times, permitted in the front section where the dancing, drinking, and live music happened and denied entry through the other doorways he saw people of influence pass through. Karam had joined him only once, pointing out those in the crowd who hid their magical strength and teaching him how to do the same as they listened to a jazz trio led by a sultry-voiced woman who resembled a young Ella Fitzgerald.

Now, though, those entering the scarlet door were hard-looking men and younger folks trying to look tough.

It seemed to have become more a clubhouse and less an entertainment venue, at least during the daylight hours. A gathering place for people committed to causing trouble, if he retained any ability to understand the streets. *Who knows, maybe it was always like that and I simply didn't see it. In any case, there's a solid chance I'll have to get in there, eventually. But it's a lousy first option.*

Tanyith leapt from the roof and used a gust of air summoned by his magic to carry him gently to the street. He ran his fingers through his shaggy beard and tugged at it as he concentrated. There were only a few people he could still trust and no guarantee that they were around or even willing. He laughed inside. *When your best option is an ex-girlfriend who dumped you, pickings are definitely slim.* With a shake of his head, he began the trek toward where she'd lived before his abduction and imprisonment.

His knowledge of the city was out of date, which denied him easy portal opportunities until he'd found locations that were secretive enough to use. His treasures were at least temporarily out of reach, and the money Nylotte had given him was dwindling quickly. The only option was a long walk. It took an hour and a half to arrive at the gorgeous neighborhood, full of grand old houses protected by high hedges. The avenue itself was idyllic with narrow cobblestone lanes separated by a wide central island of towering oak trees and pockets of bright flowers. It brought back memories, more good than bad.

He strolled slowly past the house she had lived in on the

opposite side of the street and searched for clues of her presence. The red flag with the white peace symbol on it was still suspended over the porch and blocked a part of it from view. They had spent many hours in its shade, laughing, talking, and, near the end, arguing.

She hadn't shared his concerns about his people and advocated for a life where problems were set free to be carried off by the breeze. He'd called her naïve and she'd called him territorial and power-hungry. Tanyith wasn't certain if he was totally right or if she was totally wrong. But the one thing he did know was that of all his friends, she was the only one he could be one hundred percent sure wouldn't have played a role in his abduction. *So, she's the only one I can really trust.*

The impulse almost involuntary, he picked a flower from the oasis in the center of the stone paths as he crossed them. His stomach flip-flopped as he walked up the familiar sidewalk and the sense that he'd been transported in time fourteen months back was almost overwhelming. He peered nervously left toward the shaded area, almost certain he'd see himself there, his tanned limbs wound around hers.

It was empty, but his relief was quickly shattered when the door opened. He turned his head slowly and drank in the sight of his former love where she stood in the doorway—blonde hair, tall and thin, her California childhood displayed in her sun-kissed skin, crop top, jean shorts, and bare feet. Uncertainty swept across her face followed by dawning recognition, and then she was in his arms and her tears dripped onto his shirt. "Tay, I thought you were dead. They told me you were gone."

He lowered his head to kiss the top of hers. "I was gone and I was very nearly dead. It didn't stick, though. I'm too stubborn, I guess."

She gave a choked laugh and pulled him through the door.

Chicory coffee with a dash of bourbon in it steamed before him. The kitchen hadn't changed and still gleamed with bright yellow walls and white counters. The chair he sat in was yellow vinyl with gold accents and a metal frame and matched the beaten linoleum of the wobbly table. Sienna sat across from him, cross-legged on her own seat, and sipped slowly from her own mug. He waited patiently, not wanting to break the spell or the memories of so many other moments like this one that they'd shared. *Well, not exactly like this one.*

Her tears had subsided as she'd made the drinks and now, her deep eyes stared into his. "So. What happened? No one knew."

He shook his head. "Someone knew. Someone set me up."

She nodded. "Okay. But that's not an answer."

"Yeah, I'm aware." He took a sip of his drink, winced a little at the bite of the bourbon, and cleared his throat as the liquor's heat spread in his chest. "I was more or less minding my own business. One of my people had been targeted by a couple of toughs on the street, and I was looking for clues. I hoped to not find out that it was another Atlantean but was fairly sure that was what would happen."

"So, it's a magic thing?" Her attitude toward his powers and his ancestry were the same as her attitude toward everything—live, let live, and be chill about it. It was one of the things that had drawn him to her, a classic case of seeking what you lack in another. *Hidden envy isn't the best relationship glue.*

Memories of the many other times she'd said those words inspired a small smile. "Yeah, a magic thing in part. But it's more a power thing. The strong taking advantage of the weak."

"Which, of course, you couldn't let lie, hero that you are." She grinned at yet another refrain from the past.

His expression matched hers. "Well, you know…sometimes, you have to step up."

"Not if you merely learn to be."

"I'm still too stupid."

Her laugh was the joyful chime he remembered. "Maybe it's good that some things never change. Get back to your story."

He took a deep sip of the coffee before he continued. "I was asking questions, and all I can assume is that they reached the wrong ears. Which suggests a boss of some kind, because the level of toughs we're talking about wouldn't have the pull to have me sent to Trevilsom. Hell, I can't imagine anyone in this city having that much mojo, but anything's possible." He shrugged. "So, there I was doing my thing, hitting up people I trusted for information, and everything seemed normal. I went into the Shark to chat with a few more."

Sienna interrupted, "I always loved that place."

"Me too. I guess you haven't been there lately."

"No, why?"

"It's different now. It looks like a mafia hangout from a movie or something. But back then, I thought it was safe. All I remember is going in the front door, heading to the bar, and collapsing as my body quit listening to me. Some kind of spell, I'm sure, caught me when my confidence lowered my defenses. I was rushed into the back, a bag was thrown over my head, and I lost track of things."

She shook her head. "That's insane."

"Right?" he replied with a rueful laugh. "My next moment of awareness was when the Warden at Trevilsom took possession of me. My two captors claimed I had used my magic to murder innumerable people and handed over what looked like an evidence booklet. I couldn't say anything in my own defense as my body was still locked. No one asked, either. In fact, no one spoke to me at all the entire time I was there." *Except for the screams and the whispers.*

Her face twisted in sympathy and her eyes glistened. "I'm so sorry, Tay."

With a sigh, he forced another smile. "I lived and maintained my sanity. That's what matters."

"How'd you get out?"

"That's the weird part. Someone broke me out but they weren't the ones who wanted me out. They were only hirelings. And I have no idea who that person in the background is either."

Sienna shook her head. "It's bizarre. Okay, I assume you

came to me for a reason other than to catch up. What can I do to help?"

"What's been going on while I've been gone? You know some of the people and some of the places. Have you seen anything that might be a starting point?"

She frowned as she considered the question. "Well, of your three amigos, Jackson and Dray fell off the radar right after you did. But Parker is still around. I've noticed him once or twice in the last couple of months, but not in any of the places where we used to see him—random bars, really. He's changed, though, and looks like he came into some cash. He dresses better and flashes a money clip. You know the type."

He nodded. "Okay, that's something solid. Where am I most likely to find him, do you think?"

An elegant hand with pink-painted nails lifted her cup to pale lips. His old habits were returning and top of the list was the way he'd spend minutes at a time simply watching her, entranced. "Well, you could hang around the bars where I saw him, but there's no guarantee he'll show. Maybe you should go to the Dragons instead."

Tanyith leaned back in the chair and stared at her. "I'm an idiot for not thinking of that. It could be that I didn't keep all my sanity."

Sienna laughed again. "Well, now you know." She turned serious. "Be a little more careful this time, will you?"

It was a dismissal and he couldn't fault her for wanting to get him out of her kitchen. His appearance had clearly been a shock. He stood and she rose with him. She stepped in to accept his hug. "Thanks, See."

She gave him a final squeeze and pushed him toward the exit. When he was out on the porch, she spoke quickly. "Once you've got this behind you, think about coming back to say hi." The door closed before he could answer, probably before she could catch his smile. *One more reason to get to the bottom of this garbage fast. A quick stop in the backyard to unearth my emergency cache, another to buy some decent clothes, and on to the Drunken Dragons.*

CHAPTER SIX

When Cali finally made it out of her apartment, the morning sun had given way to an afternoon shower. The walk was more enjoyable for it with an umbrella to keep her dry and the rain limiting the crowd on the sidewalks and streets. She stopped in front of the St Louis Cathedral and admired the points and spires of its gothic architecture. A small crowd had gathered nearby, most likely one of the religiously affiliated tours that seemed to somehow arrive almost every time she did.

She didn't identify as religious but harbored goodwill and vague envy for those who did. A higher power to bring one's troubles to sounded like a great idea but she hadn't found one that called to her yet. Once a month or so, she wound up at a service of some kind and tried to listen for the call that others talked about. It had yet to arrive but she never failed to enjoy the unity of purpose that resonated through the places of worship.

In a non-deific way, however, the person she was headed to visit was her higher power. Her parents had appointed Emalia as her unofficial guardian while they were alive and since their deaths, the woman had been her guide, teacher, and confidante. She had understood the young woman's need to chart her own path and offered assistance without restriction. At the same time, her mentor wasn't at all hesitant to share judgments—both good and bad—about her ward's actions. She was one of the people who invoked her full first name more often than she'd prefer. Regardless of issues of legality or age, she still thought of her parents' friend as her guardian.

Emalia held court in a modest shop along the perimeter of Jackson Square festooned with astrological symbols and a cartoonish crystal ball. Cali had watched through a spyhole from the back more than once while she used tarot cards, runes, or small bones to predict the future of those who paid for the privilege. They didn't realize the woman was magic and her insights were often accurate, although inevitably veiled. She had been the girl's sole source of magical instruction, as her parents had stubbornly refused to teach her until she reached adulthood. Fortunately, her mentor did not share their worries on that matter.

Cali checked to be sure no clients were present and pushed through the outer door. The cool interior was all black, purple, and velvet and the small round table and chairs in the center the only furniture. The room was a narrow rectangle that stretched toward the back and sounds coming from behind the heavy curtain that formed the visible back wall revealed the presence of another person.

A deep, spooky voice emanated from that direction. "Who dares to enter my domain uninvited? A doom upon you, a doom, I say!" She looked up at the almost invisible camera mounted in the rear corner of the room and extended her tongue slowly. The vocal darkness was abandoned as the other woman laughed. "Impudent whelp. Get in here."

She pushed the curtain aside and stepped into the back. Emalia lived above the shop in an equally minimalist apartment, and this area served as her living room. An electric kettle burbled happily, and she was already pulling out a tea set. Her faith in leaves and water as a key component of magic was as unflinching as her posture. She sat on the edge of a wingback leather chair and gestured for her guest to take the other. *Exactly like always.* The ritual never failed to center her mind, and in many ways, this was her true sanctuary.

"So. What brings you here today?" Her mentor's piercing gaze suggested that she already knew.

Cali played her part of the game. "Oh, nothing."

Emalia waved her hand. "Pish. If what I've heard is correct, you were in a fight. I thought I felt magical emanations that evening." The teacher was always attuned to the student, she'd said, and she had no reason to disbelieve her. It was one of the reasons that when she was truly up to something even slightly nefarious, she did it the human way.

"Yeah. It was only an idiot who turned out to have more idiots as friends."

The other woman shook her head. "Magical idiots." It wasn't a question.

She nodded. "Not so good at it, though."

The woman poured the tea from the teapot into two

cups and extended one to her. The herbal scent wafted teasingly with notes of cinnamon and anise and something that defied description and would go unnoticed by a human. She raised an eyebrow.

"Yes. It will help your magic replenish faster." *That's probably only superstition, but it* is *delicious.*

"So, what are we learning today?"

"What do you want to know?"

Cali considered before replying. "I think I need to improve my skills in illusion. They worked fine against the idiots, but there's a place I'd like to take a look at without anyone inside taking a look at me."

"You have heard of windows, right?"

She threw an overdone petulant glare at the woman and put on her patented dumb teenager voice. "They were, like, bricked up, okay?"

Her mentor's laugh was dry and brittle. "So, illusion, then. Clear your mind...."

An hour later, they were done and Cali was drained. Another round of tea and an admonition to drink it all followed, and she felt almost human—well, half-human, which meant herself—by the time it was finished. The question took her by surprise.

"Where are you going to sneak into?"

"The Shark Nightclub."

The teacup in Emalia's hand rattled against the saucer as she lowered it to the table. "That's a dangerous place. How do you know about it?"

Her look of concern demanded truth. "Dasante noticed a man watching me on the corner. I followed him for a while and that's where he wound up."

She shook her head and muttered a touch too quietly to make out what she said. Abruptly, she rose and hesitated for a moment like she was unsure of why she'd stood, then walked toward the closed door that concealed the staircase. "Come with me, Caliste."

Damn. What did I do now? She hurried after the other woman's deliberate stride. The stairs ended in her dressing area, home to a small vanity and a wardrobe. She pointed at the room's only chair and commanded, "Sit."

Cali sat. The wardrobe creaked as its door opened, and her guardian rummaged around inside, muttering under her breath again. She caught a couple of words this time, including her mother's name, and her interest ratcheted up a notch. When the other woman turned back to her, an ornate wooden box rested in her hands and a shiny golden lock dangled from the clasp. It was rectangular in the opposite direction from the apartment, more wide than long. She estimated her fingers would barely clear the top if she pressed her lower palm against the bottom edge.

The vanity was free of any clutter, as was every surface in both the public and private areas of the dwelling aside from the orb on the table downstairs. Her teacher set the box on it, positioning it so the lock was directly in front of her. Cali lifted her hand, and a sharp, "Not yet," stopped it in mid-air.

Emalia sighed. "We have reached this moment more quickly than I'd hoped and far more quickly than your parents wished. But you've been noticed despite our efforts, and so the schedule must be accelerated. You will need to come more often for training, beginning immediately."

She groaned, which drew a hint of a smile from the other woman. The warmth in her eyes as her gaze settled on her hadn't reached her voice, which was thick with concern. Cali felt like a child again, with her mother looking down at her. "What should I do?" The question was small and big—about the lock and about, well, everything.

"Wrap your hand around the lock and clear your mind." She complied and packed thoughts away the same way she did at the dojo. Her face must have shown the process because she had barely finished when Emalia spoke again. "Now, concentrate on your parents. Imagine that they are right here, in this room." The memory was painful. There had been no opportunity to say goodbye and no ceremony to mark their passing, only Emalia's caring voice telling her they'd been killed by unknown enemies according to witnesses Cali wasn't permitted to speak to. For a while, she'd believed they would reappear and simply walk into the tavern one day, but time had eroded that dream.

Words of magic floated from the other woman's lips and washed over her like a soft breeze. The lock grew warm before it clicked open. She removed it and lowered the hasp slowly. At Emalia's nod, she lifted the lid. Three objects lay inside. Two were silver rings that seemed like copies of the ones she wore on her thumbs. The other was a pendant that appeared to be identical to the one around her neck save for the lack of a chain. Her fingers were drawn to them. In fact, the items seemed to tug at her entire body. *What the hell is this?* She dragged her gaze away and looked up. "What is going on?"

The woman knelt and reached out for her hand. The contrast between her own smooth flesh and her guardian's wrinkled skin was notable and distracted her scattered mind for a moment. *My mother's would be halfway between.* Her mentor said, "You mustn't be upset about what I tell you. It was for your own good and still would be if it had succeeded in keeping you hidden. But, since it hasn't, we must adopt a different strategy."

Cali nodded. *Way to set me up to be angry.* "I'll do my best."

"The necklace and rings you wear are not merely mementos. They are magical items with a singular purpose. They've kept your magic at a level where it wouldn't be detected by those who threatened your safety —those who hunted your family after your departure from the Atlantean homeland."

The words didn't register. "Are you saying they disguise my power?" She'd always considered her magic above average, not necessarily in absolute strength but in its ability to be used in so many different ways.

Emalia sighed. "No, I'm saying they suppress it. Child, you are far more powerful than you think you are." Again, she reached for the items and again, the older woman stopped her. "Taking them now would do you no good. A ritual is required. We will meet at the threshold between today and tomorrow in St Louis One."

Cali's brain began to spin. She'd been deceived—arguably for her own benefit and by people she loved and trusted—but she absolutely hated being lied to. Emalia's warning made perfect sense since she was well aware of her opinions on that issue. She rose abruptly and headed to the stairs. Softer footsteps followed her, and as she pushed aside the curtain to move toward the entrance, a soft voice trailed after. "Your feelings are valid, Caliste, but do not forget that you don't yet know everything. This wasn't a choice made without ample cause."

She didn't slam the door, which felt like a victory of restraint. Her feet guided her toward the tavern while her mind chewed on a single question. *How in the world could having* less *magical ability be safer than having more?*

CHAPTER SEVEN

Zeb yelled, "Cali, where's your damn brain, girl?" His gruff voice carried across to where she gathered the pile of bar rags she'd dropped.

She lifted them, careful to extend a particular finger in a way he'd notice, and evaded two drunk wizards who waved wands about before they stowed them on the shelf under the bar. "You're probably not high up enough to see it. I could get you another crate to stand on."

His glare was betrayed by the upward quirk at the corners of his lips, and she grinned as she turned to stare at the main room. Sunday nights weren't the busiest, so there were spaces at the tables here and there and the tall seats running along the bar were only half-full.

He had noticed her preoccupation when she'd arrived and acknowledged it with the tilt of his head but had respectfully not pushed her on it. That hadn't prevented the almost constant flow of comments about her missing mind, though. If her count was correct, they'd now reached double digits in only a couple of hours.

Her quick gaze searched the crowd for troublemakers, happy to find that none of the usual suspects—or unusual suspects, as Dasante described them when he occasionally hung out during her shifts—were present. *Finally, maybe I can have a relaxing evening in this place. Heaven knows I need to get a handle on the fact that I'm meeting my mentor in a cemetery at midnight and that's only the smallest part of the weirdness to come.*

The door slammed against the wall to signal the entry of someone who hadn't been to the Drunken Dragons Tavern enough times to know better. About a third of the crowd turned, as did Zeb. Her gaze had already been on the entrance, so she saw the woman before any of the others did. She seemed of average height with short black hair swept to one side, tanned skin, a sleek and shiny brown leather jacket over a dark green blouse, blue jeans, and fashionable boots that matched the coat.

She moved like someone who spent time at the gym, direct and powerful, and as she approached, a twist of the hips revealed the gold badge on her belt. Cali turned to Zeb, but he had his gaze locked on the detective. He waited, though, and made her come to him. The curve of her lips when she reached the bar showed that she'd noticed.

"Are you Zarden?" Her voice was pleasant and matter-of-fact, neither hopeful nor doubtful. Cali pegged her in her late twenties, but she had the kind of angular features that made it difficult to be certain. Her green eyes were sharp and intense.

"I am. And who are you, door-banger?"

The woman gave a thin smile. "Detective Kendra

Barton, NOPD Specialized Investigations." She paused for a reaction and finding none, continued. "I'm looking into an incident the other night that's been linked to your business." She drew a small notebook from her back pocket and flipped it open. "Someone named Jarten was attacked on the street after leaving here."

A sharp glance from Zeb cut Cali's angry denial off, and she covered her instinctive flinch by reaching for a cloth to wipe the bar. The dwarf nodded. "We know Jarten. He's in here every week or so. It's not a huge shock that his stupidity got him into a scrape since his mouth is far bigger than his brain. You didn't say you were homicide, so I presume the troublemaker is still among the living?"

"Last time I checked. So, you confirm that he was here?"

Her boss shrugged. "Sure. He was here. Then he left."

Barton raised an eyebrow. "And you have nothing more to report on the topic?"

"The customer experience ends at the door, Detective. You're welcome to hang around the place for more information. You look like someone who works for a living, so if you want to help me tend bar—you know, undercover—it could be a win for both of us."

It earned him a laugh edged with disbelief. "Well, Zarden, as much as I appreciate the offer, I think I'll have to decline for now." She closed the notebook and returned it to its home before she turned her gaze to Cali. "Hopefully, this isn't an insensitive question. Do you speak?"

The girl broke into laughter. "Yes, I speak. But I don't like to pre-empt my boss. He's sensitive about that kind of thing."

The detective gave her a blank-faced stare. It was a

familiar technique, often required when dealing with customers, so it failed to impress. Cali held a fourth-dan black belt where that skill was concerned. "So, do you know anything about the person of interest?"

"Jarten?" she asked, knowing Barton hadn't forgotten his name.

"Yes," the woman responded, clearly knowing Cali was trying to tweak her.

"Sure. He's a terrible tipper, smells like a flower, and can't handle his alcohol."

Barton shook her head. "I'm not really concerned about his choice of cologne. Do you have anything useful for me with regard to the alleged assault?" She paused, a look of uncertainty on her face, and retrieved the notebook again and paged through it. "Right, I thought I remembered that. It says here that the eyewitness reported it was a woman who did the beat-down. A woman with red hair."

Zeb's voice interrupted. "Well, hell, Detective, any Irish person worth their Guinness would be able to smack that twiggy jerk."

She chuckled but didn't release the eye-lock she had put on Cali. "I couldn't help but notice you're a woman with red hair."

"One of many."

"But the only one who has a clear connection to Jarten and to the Dragons." She gestured to indicate the building around them.

Cali's mind perked up. *She must have heard someone refer to the Tavern that way. I wonder if it's Jarten who is behind this?* "The only one you know of so far. I'm afraid you'll have to keep detecting, detective. There's nothing to see here." She mimicked the other woman's gesture.

With a chuckle, Barton put the notebook away again. "Sure, Caliste. That is your name, right? I did do a little detecting before I arrived."

She let her glower provide the answer, and the woman laughed. "Okay, then. If you think of anything else that might be useful, feel free to stop at the station on Wednesday. I'm off for the next couple of days. Maybe I'll spend some time here."

Cali put a hand on her hip. "We're happy to serve whatever types come through here, Detective. We don't discriminate. Although we do prefer those who don't slam the door."

The woman pivoted quickly and looked at Zeb. "Perhaps you should be a little more discerning so trouble won't find you."

The bartender nodded slowly. "It's always good to avoid trouble. But sometimes, first impressions aren't accurate and you don't know who'll turn out to be friend or foe." He smiled suddenly. "Would you like a drink for the road, officer?"

She laughed again and shook her head, the short black hair fluttering with the movement. "Thanks. How about a rain check?"

"Done. You're always welcome, Kendra Barton."

She headed to the door but stopped before opening it. Without turning, she said, "Caliste, let's make that an official appointment for Wednesday. See you at the Royal Street station at one?"

Cali looked at Zeb and received a nod. "Fine. One." The detective waved as she departed.

Once she'd circulated through the room to ensure everyone was taken care of, Cali took a seat on one of the high chairs across from the dwarf. He put a glass of ice in front of her and filled it with Cherry Coke from the bar's soda gun. She drank deeply, then sighed. "So, do you think I'm in trouble?"

He pulled the tall chair that sat next to the back wall forward and clambered up onto it. "Maybe so. Maybe not. But what's important is how you'll deal with it."

She shook her head. "Has anyone ever told you that your answers aren't always particularly useful?"

"Other than you? Never." The overly innocent expression on his face was a sure sign of a lie.

"How do you get Zeb out of Zarden, anyway?" She'd been surprised to discover he had another name.

He continued as if she hadn't asked. "So, what are your thoughts about the situation?"

"There are a couple of possibilities. One, Jarten is behind it, but he thinks that not calling me out by name will keep his involvement hidden. Or maybe a random witness, but anyone who knows those four would probably be celebrating, not summoning the police. My money's on the first."

Zeb ran his fingers through his perfectly maintained black beard and revealed a strand or two of grey. She pushed away the desire to tease him about it. *Age gets almost everybody, eventually. I'll stick to short jokes.* He nodded. "I'm with you. He's behind it."

"Maybe I shouldn't have fought them over a bar tab?"

He shook his head. "The little jerk broke the rules. Tell me, if he'd asked to keep a tab running, would we have let him?"

"Of course." They did that all the time. Wizards, in particular, could be counted on to always remember their wands and frequently forget everything else.

"If he'd requested a loan, would you have given him one?"

She had to think about that one. "Yeah, I suppose. Once, at least. I'm not exactly flush. Hey, maybe you could pay me more and I could afford to give loans? Make the customers happy?"

The dwarf chuckled. "Or maybe you could work more and earn yourself more money."

It was a long-standing joke and mostly fell flat under the concerns of the moment. "So I was right to fight over it?"

He leaned back with a smile that peeked out from under the black—and ever so slightly grey—mustache. "That's not for me to answer, Caliste. Each of us is our own judge. Were you?"

Thoughtfully, she tapped her fingers slowly on the bar as she replayed the incident. *He had options but he chose to break the rules of hospitality of the tavern. I didn't fight until I could talk first. I tried to defuse the situation but they escalated it. On the other hand, I could have walked away and paid the bill myself.* She rejected that idea as quickly as it appeared. *No. That might have solved the immediate problem but it wouldn't have addressed the violation. It isn't right to dine and dash on your host.*

"I was. We're living in a society here, damn it. You don't

do junk like that."

His head lowered and rose once. "Agreed."

Warmth flooded through her at his words. She knew she put too much stock in them and didn't care. He, Emalia, and Sensei Ikehara were her role models and guides now, and she treasured each of them. "But I could have tried to talk again after the first one went down."

Zeb leaned forward to light his pipe and take a drag, then returned it to its holder under the bar. He expelled a series of perfect smoke rings before he answered. "I believe your heart is in the right place. Those are questions you should ask, always. It's good to learn from your experiences." He grinned. "But Jarten and his friends earned their reward. I don't think you were excessive. If anything, breaking a limb on each of the morons would have kept them out of our hair longer."

She laughed. "Wise words from a wise person. But if that's what you think, why weren't you the one to chase after them?"

He raised an eyebrow. "Dwarves are made for sprints, not marathons. We're deadly over short distances but tend to throw axes at fleeing enemies to avoid long runs."

There was a clatter from behind, and she rolled her eyes. "Maybe an ax would have been the right solution."

"It might have killed him. And that would have been..." He paused. "Overkill."

With a heartfelt groan at the Dad joke, she turned away from the bar and aimed herself toward the part of the room the unwelcome breaking sounds had emanated from. *I can't spend any more time here than I already do. The bad jokes would kill me dead.*

CHAPTER EIGHT

S*aint Louis Cemetery One, home of Voodoo notable Marie Laveau, future resting place of Nicolas Cage, and proud owner of one damn annoying wall.* Cali had been inside many times but always with Dasante's helping hands to boost her in return for hauling him up after. It hadn't felt right to bring him along tonight.

She'd managed to ignore her anger at the deceptions for most of the evening by keeping busy at the tavern and had stayed after the end of her shift to clean up unasked. The task effectively filled the hours between closing and her appointment among the dead. A quick walk brought her there with ten minutes to spare, living up to her father's cheerfully delivered motto of, "Early is on time and on time is late."

However, she'd failed to account for the brick and cement barrier that surrounded the graveyard. The bricks were dangerous and prone to crumble underfoot—at the behest of the ghosts within, said the superstitious. She wasn't sure about the second part but had verified the first personally and didn't have any desire to scrape the skin left bare by her tanktop trying to climb it.

She'd chosen the section with the smallest number of sightlines to try a new form of magic. Emalia had explained a few weeks before that others used force to create magical versions of mundane items, such as swords or whips. Cali hadn't had an opportunity to work with the idea yet thanks to her heavy schedule. She shut away irrelevant thoughts one by one until she had a pure mind and envisioned a set of blocks leading up to the wall. She shaped them with her hands, pictured them coming into being, and felt the itching on her arms that signaled energy flowing from her.

The steps were visible only as a wavering translucence, and she climbed them quickly while she struggled to maintain the flow of power. When she reached the top, she allowed them to evaporate. She nodded to acknowledge her success, lowered herself to hang from the wall by her fingertips, and dropped to the roof of one of the vaults. A quick jump took her safely down to the graveled path.

Storage of the departed in New Orleans was exclusively in above-ground structures, as digging even a couple of feet down revealed soggy earth from the high water table. Emalia hadn't specified where they'd meet inside, but the choice was obvious. A few turns and a short straight path took her to a far corner where a vault with the family name Leblanc lay. It wasn't her family's as such, but it was where her parents were interred, placed there under cover of darkness by Emalia and friends. Or so she'd been told since she hadn't been permitted to be there when it happened.

It doesn't matter, really. Wherever they are, they're watching over me if they can. One place is the same as the next. Her guardian's thin form, standing with her perfect posture as always, emerged from the gap between vaults. "Caliste. Are you well?"

She realized there were tears on her cheeks and dashed them away with a knuckle. "Fine. Good. Soon to be great, right? Let's get on with it."

The other woman nodded and began to chant softly as she gestured with her long-sleeved arms in time with the melody. It wasn't quite a song but also wasn't quite not a song. When she finished, the world seemed to grow more distant. *There's an illusion of some kind around us. She must be worried about discovery.*

Emalia opened the flap of the embroidered cloth satchel that hung from a narrow diagonal strap across her chest and withdrew three pouches. From the first two, she withdrew the silver rings that had been in the treasure box and from the last, the pendant that matched the one she wore.

She beckoned Cali forward, and she obeyed and extended her hands. Thin fingers pushed the rings onto her thicker index fingers with the admonition, "Do not let them touch." She nodded and kept her thumbs stretched away. The new items fit perfectly as if they'd been made specifically for that moment in time. When the others had grown tight, Emalia had used magic to enlarge them. The woman reached for the pendant around her neck and pressed the other one to the back of it, flat side against flat side. A thin layer of white adhesive was visible and held them together while it prohibited the metal from touching.

Satisfied, she nodded and stepped backward. "For this

to work properly, you must understand a few things first. I will explain. You may ask questions but I do not promise to answer all of them."

"Okay."

Her eyes narrowed at the tone but she didn't otherwise point out Cali's snarkiness. "You were too young to remember when your parents fled New Atlantis, following other refugees who had arrived in this city. At that time, Atlanteans in exile were one people, although that quickly changed. While your mother and father were alive, they undertook to mask your power so you—and they—wouldn't be discovered. When the searchers came, year after year, they were able to hide well enough to avoid them." She paused.

Cali asked, "Why didn't they tell me any of this?"

Emalia nodded. "A reasonable question. Two reasons. First, like all parents, they didn't want their child to worry about things beyond her control. Second, they didn't want to prejudice you against your people until you were experienced enough to differentiate between the competing groups."

"Okay." This time, the response was less snarky and more understanding. She was trying.

The older woman sighed. "Their plan was to keep your power under control themselves, increasing it only as you learned to master it and more importantly, learned how to mask it yourself. When signs appeared indicating the search for your family had intensified, they were forced to choose a different option." Cali waggled her fingers and received a nod. "A set of items magicked to suppress and conceal your magic until the threat had ended."

"Has it?" She ignored the growing urge to clink the rings together.

"Sadly, no. There was one other condition we agreed would require removing the protection. When you told me an Atlantean was watching you and that he entered that particular establishment, it was clear that you'd been noticed. The time for concealment has ended."

"Who were we hiding from?"

"Those who would wish you harm." She raised a hand. "Some things are not important tonight. I will share them with you on another occasion. About what I've said, is there anything that's still unclear?"

Cali considered it and decided that if her mentor felt it wasn't important, she'd trust her judgment. She shook her head.

"Do you understand why your parents felt they must conceal this from you and why they had to take actions to prevent discovery?"

She nodded.

The woman's tone lowered and when the words emerged, they carried twice as much weight as anything Emalia had ever said to her, including breaking the news of her parents' deaths. "Do you forgive them?"

A child's voice inside screamed, *No, never.* She closed her eyes and sent sympathy and understanding to her familiar passenger, the part of her who still couldn't cope with her parents' involuntary abandonment. Once she was soothed, she could think. *Would I keep things secret to protect someone less powerful than me if I thought it was in their best interests? Yeah, I would. Great power, great responsibility, and all that.*

The child insisted, *but they left me.* Cali shook her head. *They didn't want to. They did what was best for us. And we have to forgive them for not being perfect.* She opened her eyes and looked squarely at her guardian. "I do."

A tone of vulnerability she'd never heard from the other woman suffused her next question. "Can you forgive me?"

The answer required zero thought. "No. There is nothing to forgive. Instead, I thank you for honoring their wishes and standing in their place when they no longer could." She pushed tears back. *Stupid emotions.*

Relief flickered across Emalia's features but was quickly banished and only a grave expression remained as the older woman spoke. "Then it is time for you to receive your true inheritance. Push that love and forgiveness to the front of your mind and when it is as full as you can make it, tap the rings together and say *Apokalupto.*"

Cali mentally recited the word twice to cement it into memory, drew in a deep breath, and closed her eyes again. She thought of the best moments with her parents, the ones she cherished and only brought forward in celebration or in great need. Layer upon layer, they filled her consciousness until all she could sense was love tempered by loss but free of blame. Finally, she spoke the word and the world exploded.

She was jolted back to her senses by the sound of Emalia's scream. "Caliste, wake up. Fight or it will kill you!"

CHAPTER NINE

Cali scrambled back as the world tilted and spun crazily in her vision. Her body trembled and jolted in reaction to the magic that coursed through it. Pleasure followed pain and was succeeded by pain again in fast flashes. She collided with a solid wall and pushed her way up it as she squeezed her eyes shut and opened them again in an effort to bring something—anything—into focus.

When her eyes cleared, the monster in front of her was so unbelievable that she shook her head furiously to see if it would disappear. It didn't but instead, poked its snout at the figure of her guardian, who was locked inside a shimmering magical cocoon that hovered an inch away from her skin. The creature turned its head toward her and revealed vertically slitted black pupils in irises of orange and gold over an elongated snout filled with teeth.

Its body was sinuous and strong, supported by four legs. A foot of space was visible between its belly and the ground, and Cali estimated it would rise to three feet along its back, possibly four with its long neck extended. Right now, that neck was stretched as the beast swayed toward her and its thick tail flicked from side to side with each step. Soft snorts emerged from its nostrils.

She pushed away from the wall, encouraged to discover she still possessed a measure of balance and stability as she sank into an aikido stance. Her lead foot now rested forward and the rear one at a ninety-degree angle with her weight centered. She lifted her front hand with the palm out. "Hey now, mister or miss, or whatever…uh, dragon, lizard…thing." *Great start, Cali. Offend it right off the bat.* "There's no need for this. In the immortal words of Will Smith, 'My attitude is don't start nothin, won't be nothin'." His advance paused as if he considered her suggestion but was clearly unmoved as he glided into motion again. "Okay, this is your last chance to avoid getting yourself hurt."

The creature snarled, and she resisted the urge to retreat from the harsh sound. Her body began to feel like her own again, but different. Where before, her magic had seemed to lie in her core waiting to be drawn out for use, it now suffused her as if every cell had a new spark of power inside it. The moonlight shone upon the beast's scales as it continued to advance, some of which seemed reflective and some not. She pointed. "Hey. You. Are you listening?"

It settled into a seated position like a cat and curled its tail around its body. *Good, maybe we're getting somewhere.* For a second, it appeared ready to sneeze and its snout lowered before it raised again with an open mouth, the sharp teeth obvious and alarming. They weren't as scary as the blast of sparkling mist that spewed out of its maw toward her, though.

Cali motioned quickly with her hand and a curved force shield materialized before her. The mist turned to ice on its surface and the rest flowed around her without effect. She stared at her arms, which were covered with unfamiliar arcane shapes and symbols glowing in fluorescent blue, green, gold, and orange. The creature closed its mouth, and the new markings faded with the shield.

"Okay. You had to try. I get it. I'll give you that. But if you do it again, we'll definitely tussle. I don't know who you are. Hell, I don't know what you are. But we can call this done." She'd cast shields before but never so easily or with such stability. The lizard tilted his head like he understood her words but charged without warning.

She stilled as it surged in and defocused her eyes to see its whole body the way Sensei Ikehara had taught her. Sure enough, the rush was a feint, and it stopped and pivoted to strike from the side with its tail. It was an attempt to sweep her ankles, and she skipped over it with ease, circled away from it to lead the tail's reverse slash, and forced the creature to keep turning to try to acquire her. She was loath to go on the offensive for any number of reasons. The beast was amazing, her kicks and punches probably wouldn't work against it, and she wasn't certain she could control her magic sufficiently to wound and not kill. Finally, the child within squealed with the desire to become friends and play with it.

Rather than press any kind of advantage, she retreated, which allowed the creature to finish its turn and face her. Before she could speak it attacked again with its head down and on a direct trajectory. *Okay, buddy. So be it.* When it came close, she jumped first to the left to make it miss, then to the right as she hurled her body upward to wrap her arms around his neck. She held on and her momentum flipped him over. His thrashing was too fierce for her to maintain her hold, and she scrambled away. He locked fiery eyes on her and she knew he was planning to breathe at her again. *Nope. Not going to happen.*

She slammed her closed fists together in front of her and the silver rings on her thumbs rang as they collided. Each hand made a downward curve in the opposite direction to create a shimmering half-circle in the air. It streaked forward and left a trail as it passed over the creature's back, and its breath struck the half-cylinder of force as it snapped shut. The lizard banged against the surfaces surrounding it halfheartedly before it lowered onto its haunches and stared at her. Its snout moved weirdly and a strange muffled huffing reached her ears. *Wait a minute. Is it laughing at me?*

Cali put her hands on her hips and glared at it. "Are you laughing at me, you little...you little...uh, whatever?" Its snout lowered in what was clearly a nod. "So you totally can understand me." Another nod confirmed it. "Fine. Let Emalia go." It twisted its head to her guardian and the shimmering dissipated. The older woman stumbled forward and hurried across to her.

"Are you okay, Caliste?"

"Never better. What the hell is that thing and why did it attack me?"

Emalia walked around it, and the creature seemed pleased to be admired. It showed no sign that being held captive bothered it. "I never imagined I'd see one. When I left New Atlantis, all the adults had died and the next generation were still in their eggs. It's a Draksa." She said it reverentially.

"Awesome. And a Draksa is what?"

"The best way to describe them is a cross between a lizard and a dragon. Some are more of one, while some are more of the other. When the dragon side is ascendant, they are fiercely intelligent. When the lizard side is dominant, they are less smart but far more aggressive."

Cali laughed. "So this is probably one of the dumb ones, then?" She was shocked to see both Emalia and the creature in the cylinder glare at her. "What?"

"If it had wanted to kill you, it could have done it before you had a chance to react. Both of us, actually. The fact that it didn't suggests it had something else in mind. Thus, it's intelligent."

That inspired a frown. "Attacking me is a weird way to say hi."

The older woman shrugged. "Perhaps it was testing you to see how you'd react. Maybe, if you'd tried to kill it instead of trying to talk, it would have killed you outright."

She turned to the creature. "So, can we call a truce here?" His mouth parted in something that looked like a smile—a very sharp toothy smile. *This is a bad idea.* She let the power fall away and the Draksa stood and shook itself. It had kept its wings in during the short battle but unfurled them now to flick dirt from its scales.

Her guardian moved to stand beside her and watch. "They change genders more than once during their lifetime for unknown reasons. This one is between. You can tell by the scales. Metallic and shiny are male, to attract a mate. Matte is female because we don't need to show off."

"So how do I refer to it?"

"I have no idea. You'll have to ask the Draksa."

Cali shook her head. "Why is it here?"

"Again, I have no idea. You'll have to ask the Draksa."

She laughed. "Is that the only thing you'll say for the rest of the night?" As the first syllable came out, she put a hand over her mentor's mouth. "Okay, thanks, I got it. You can toddle along now."

Emalia chuckled. "Oh, there's no chance of that. I can't wait to see what happens."

The girl rolled her eyes. "Can I get you popcorn? Soda?"

"If you would, that would be lovely."

Sigh. She approached the dragon lizard and knelt in the dirt before it so her eyes were level with its own. "I'm Cali." It nodded and seemed to be waiting. "Um, are you here because of me specifically?" It nodded again. "Because of the spell we cast?" She lifted the necklace to show the pendants and blinked in surprise at the discovery that they had become a single two-sided object with no visible seam.

The creature tilted its head to the side. She took that as the Draksa version of "meh." With a frown, she tried again. "Did the spell itself summon you magically?" It shook its head. "Did you notice the magic, then? Were you here?" A nod. "You live in the cemetery?" Another nod.

She twisted to shoot a glare at Emalia. "Seriously, will you be of any use at all?"

The woman chuckled. "Try asking it if it plans to come home with you."

Cali laughed at first, then realized she was serious. "Uh, right. Sure. Tonight is already beyond weird, so why not?" She turned to the creature. Its gaze locked on hers and the depths of them stole her breath for a minute. "Okay, Draksa. Would you like to come home with me? My apartment is small but we can find a way to make it work. I imagine it'll be better than living here."

It nodded, looked regal, and pushed onto its feet with a flutter of wings, obviously ready to depart. She stood as well. "May I…uh, touch you?" It nodded again. She put her hand on its back and felt its intentions clearly—the pineapple taste of goodwill tempered with the faint lingering cinnamon burn that conveyed mischievousness. At the moment of contact, her arms had begun to glow and the neon of her magical markings spread out to its scales until their colors matched. She hissed a sharp intake of breath. "Whoa."

Emalia's voice from behind her was reverential. "You're bonded. It offered magic, and yours was accepted. I've only ever heard about it in fairy tales as the bondings of the last generation of Draksa happened before my time."

She turned in alarm. "What does that mean?"

Her mentor shook her head with an incredulous laugh as if she couldn't believe it either. "Till death do you part, Caliste."

Cali's mouth dropped open but as it was only one in a chain of incredible events for the day, it didn't overwhelm her. "Awesome." She spun to face the creature. "Do you want to be called he and him, since there's a touch more metal on your scales?" It made the laughing sound again and bobbed its snout. "Fine. I always imagined having a cat named Whiskers but somehow, I think you'd see a cat more as a snack than a friend. So, how about I call you that instead?"

He glared at her, and she wracked her brain for other names. "Skittles." His snout shifted from side to side. "Midnight." He twisted his head to indicate his brilliant scales. "Got it. Fyre."

After a moment's consideration, he nodded and turned to walk toward the exit, clearly expecting her to follow. *I'll never be able to tell anyone about this day. Even Dasante would lock me in a padded room for my own good. And then Fyre would eat the key.*

CHAPTER TEN

Tanyith was back on the roof across from The Shark Nightclub. His purpose there was to watch those who came and went and note who talked to who before they vanished into the building's hidden interior. His scrying tricks had been defeated by the establishment's defensive wards. He'd known it would have such protections but had still needed to make the attempt and had covered his tracks carefully to avoid being backtracked.

The patterns were familiar, the same as when he'd been part of the Atlantean gang working out of a different club. But in his day, they'd gone out to watch over the streets and to look for newcomers and help them acclimate. Admittedly, they'd skirted the edges of the law to pull money away from those who made it with gambling and homemade alcohol and the occasional grift on wealthy tourists, but nothing like what was happening now.

He'd spent his waking hours following the street soldiers for two days, and he was reasonably sure he had a good grasp of the operation. Cash was laundered through the nightclub and it served as the gang's base of operations. Tendrils extended from this hub through the city for three purposes he'd identified. First—and still—gambling. Second, homemade alcohol he took no issue with, and illegal drugs he absolutely did have a problem with. Third, and most concerning, they were running a protection racket. It was obvious from the looks of the shop owners as they peered after the gang members to ensure the soldiers had departed and to see who else might be under their thumb.

The new crew was engaged in all the things he had campaigned against in the old one, constantly fighting and refighting the same uphill battle. While he was away, his side had lost. It wasn't hard to imagine there was some cause and effect in play. Or, more accurately, some "getting the troublemaker out of the way before we do what we're going to do." Surveillance was the only investigative tool he had at the moment but so far, he hadn't recognized anyone among those entering or leaving.

There seemed to be a different group of people handling each of the gang's efforts. The toughest ones strong-armed shop owners and the weakest spread through the city to gather bets. If it was anything like a couple of years before, wagers would be accepted on everything from the Saints score to the number of drunks who would collapse unconscious on the unforgiving concrete of Bourbon street in a given timeframe.

When a set of toughs emerged, he followed. An hour of preparation had acquainted him with the rooftops and how they connected, and it only took an occasional burst of magic to carry him over the gaps he couldn't jump. It would work until they reached a main cross-street or residential district when he'd have to descend and be more careful. He was confident in his ability to keep track of them and only slightly less assured of being able to deal with them if things went awry.

They'd almost reached Canal street, the Southwest boundary of the French Quarter, when the four Atlanteans stopped suddenly, blocked by an equal number of men who looked fully human. Tanyith crouched and whispered a spell that would bring their words to him.

The biggest human was clearly the leader. He stood ahead of the others with his arms folded over his chest. The most notable thing about him was the fact that he wore a suit in the New Orleans heat, as did the rest of his people. One of the Atlanteans, notably not the biggest, stepped forward to meet him and they exchanged nods before the human spoke.

"You'll have to turn back, friend. Everything east of Canal is ours."

The Atlantean laughed. "No chance. The quarter's disputed territory. You know this. I know this. Hell, my grandmother knows this, and she's not even in the game."

His counterpart shrugged. "If you continue, your personal safety cannot be assured."

Another laugh followed. "When is it ever? You choose to play, you choose the risks. The same goes for you, friend."

The humans spread out a little, ready for whatever came next, and the Atlanteans mirrored them. The two spokespeople merely stared at one another. Finally, the suited man nodded. "Your call. I've passed the message as I was instructed to do. I will let Mr Grisham know of your response and I'm sure he'll have his own to share with you in the near future."

Tanyith watched the humans move away with the acrid taste of fear in the back of his throat. His gang had always—always—been smart enough to respect the streets claimed by the long-established crime boss of New Orleans. The encounter meant that one or the other of the gangs, and perhaps some of the smaller ones in town, were pushing to expand their territory. *Damn. This could blow up into a war for control of the city.*

Even dazed by the alarming revelations, he'd managed to follow them on foot without betraying his surveillance. They made a few stops along the way but appeared to be headed somewhere in particular. A drink here, a conversation there, and maybe a cash pickup at a souvenir shop, but they seemed like waypoints leading to a definite destination.

They emerged from the quarter as the sun surrendered and night spread across the streets. He lost sight of them when they turned an unfamiliar corner and when he followed, the street was empty. Irritated, he looked up at an old-fashioned wooden sign with dragons on it and shook his head. The tavern had been there in his day, but his gang had stayed away from it, even for socialization. Rumor had it that the bartender was not someone you messed with if you wanted to keep all your limbs intact, and every tale was bigger than the next. Still, it seemed like fate had lent a hand to bring him to the place he'd planned to visit anyway.

Tanyith took a deep breath and pushed the door open. It banged against the wall and made him cringe. He shook his head sheepishly at all the annoyed faces that turned his way. The entrance was in a corner and directly ahead was a sturdy polished wood bar that curved on both ends. High seats were strung along it. Behind them was a large room filled with long wooden tables butted up against each other with a mismatch of chairs and stools and benches on either side. Arched doorways with bead curtains were set left, middle, and right on the back wall.

Beyond the far end of the bar, there seemed to be a walled-off space that held a kitchen or storage or something. On the near end, a dwarven face stared at him and watched him survey the area. He crossed to take the seat across from the impressively bearded fellow. "Hey."

"Hey yourself. Welcome to the Drunken Dragons Tavern, first-timer. What'll ya have?"

"Dealer's choice."

The dwarf nodded, selected a short, curved glass, and filled it from a small cask that sat at his right hand. He placed the drink on the bar—amber with a thin layer of foam. "This is a sipping beer. My own recipe."

Tanyith took a sip as was expected and immediately began to cough as the combination of alcohol and spice attacked his body. It was completely unlike anything he'd ever tasted and when he recovered, the bartender was grinning. "It takes some getting used to. You did well for a first try."

He wiped his eyes and nodded. "Thanks. I think."

"I'm Zeb. This is my place. You're welcome here."

"Good to know." He felt like he'd passed a test. "Can I ask you a question?"

The proprietor grinned. "Right after you've paid for your drink."

With a laugh, he handed a ten over and got four back, which was a damn bargain for both the city and the quality of what he'd received. "Did a few street punks with delusions of adequacy come in a few minutes before I did?"

A snort came from his right and a female voice said, "Oh yeah, this guy will fit in perfectly at the Dragons. You sound exactly like Zeb." He turned to see striking red hair and once he got past that, realized it was the person he'd seen outside The Shark a couple of days before.

"Hey."

She rolled her eyes. "Not good at talking to girls, huh? That's fine. Neither is Zeb." She spun away to respond to a customer, and he looked back to find the dwarf shaking his head.

Tanyith heard long-suffering and fond pride in his words. "She's something, that one."

"Clearly. So, the toughs?"

Zeb pointed with his chin. Tanyith followed the line to the far wall of the room where the foursome sat. He swiveled back to the bar, took another sip of his drink, and relished the burn now that he knew to expect it. *There's more than enough time to deal with them after.* "Regulars?"

"Nah. I've seen 'em in here once or twice, tops. Do you have some business with them?"

"You might say that, I suppose. Or maybe I do. I don't know yet."

The bartender's eyebrows dipped to make a V pointed at his nose. "We welcome all kinds here. There's no discrimination as long as everyone follows the rules. That includes those who think others aren't following a rule that's important to them."

He smiled. *Could be those tales weren't all only words.* "Understood. I can't speak for those boys, but I only want to talk. I think, though, that they might be here to talk to the owner if you know what I mean."

The dwarf nodded. "We get visits from all sides now and again. I treat 'em to a drink, tell 'em they're welcome to come here but so is everyone else, and that Valerie is all the protection I need." He gestured at the battleax hung over the bar, which Tanyith had noticed about a second and a half after entering. "So, they go away until the next one thinks they have a better argument."

"Do you have a sense of who has claimed what turf?"

He shrugged. "Nope. And I don't care much. No one messes with me and I don't mess with anyone. Live and let live."

The next sip of the beer went down smoother, and his body was unanimous in its appreciation from head to stomach. "I really wish I could be like you. But some wrongs require righting."

The bartender stroked his beard. "Ah, so you've been wronged, have you?"

"You could say that."

"By those in the corner?"

He pursed his lips in thought. "Not specifically. But I'm very sure they're part of it. At the very least, they're the next step in finding out who's responsible."

"You seem like you're okay now. Is it really worth it?" The server's voice was startling when she spoke from behind him. *This beer is clearly more powerful than it seems. I'd better stop.* "He does this with everyone. It's easiest to avoid eye contact and back away slowly."

They all laughed, and Tanyith rose. His stance was solid and he was thankful for the woman's interruption. He pointed a finger the dwarf. "Don't think I'm unaware of what you were doing, you subtle saboteur."

Zeb grinned. "Peace, friend. Ideally, for everyone."

He rotated carefully to face the common room and located his targets, who talked loudly and gestured expansively in the corner. "That's always my first choice. Sadly, some fools won't play along."

The voice of reason from behind the bar followed him as he walked through the crowd. "Who's the bigger fool, then?"

Tanyith shook his head to brush the challenge off. He arrived unnoticed and tapped the one who had stepped forward as leader earlier on the shoulder. "Hey, buddy, can I ask you a question?"

CHAPTER ELEVEN

At a chin tilt from Zeb, Cali paralleled the stranger one row over as he headed to the group in the corner. *Too bad I had to leave Fyre in my room. I'm sure he could diffuse any situation he wanted to.* She laughed at the image of the rottweiler-sized Draksa standing on a table in the middle of the Tavern and covering everyone with ice. *I could yell "everyone chill" beforehand. It'd be perfect.* What wasn't perfect was the seated man's reaction to being tapped on the shoulder.

The cowl of his hoodie spun outward as he launched to his feet and stood nose to nose with the stranger. "Who's asking?"

She was an expert at using a smile as an instigation, and she heard the telltale of the tactic in his voice. "I'll take that as permission. I'm John. John Doe. I wondered if you'd care to tell me who's in charge of your little gang."

"I am. Now, step away before you end up with that name on your toe tag."

Cali moved around the table and put her back against

the wall so she could see their faces. The stranger didn't look even remotely worried. "I'd be happy to do so, but I really need that answer first."

"You won't get it." The other three men rose to their feet as well, and she said a silent thanks to the universe that this group hadn't been allowed to run a tab, unlike Jarten.

"Would you care to continue the discussion outside?" The stranger jerked his head toward the door.

"Let's do it here." The gang leader drew a fist back and she slid smoothly between them to grab and pinch each of their near arms as she shouted, "Stop." Both men gave tiny yelps.

She tasted black licorice and ash from the street tough. He was ready to fight. The stranger was lemon with a touch of anise, a testament to his determination and willingness to back it up with force. She glared at the man to her right. "You've been here before. You know better than to mix it up inside. Don't make Zeb take Valerie down." She looked at the stranger, who up close and from the front was more attractive than she'd realized. The dirty brown pompadour and beard seemed less scraggly from this angle—more like a Viking than the poser she'd categorized him as on the first impression. "You get the benefit of the doubt. No fighting in here. Period. Either settle with words or head outside."

The thug shoved her hand away and pushed past toward the door. The stranger stepped aside and watched the others file out after their leader, carbon copies in dirty jeans and dark hoodies. He shrugged and gave her a half-smile. "I didn't get my answer. I guess I have to go ask again."

She shook her head. "Zeb would say you don't need to."

"He'd be wrong. The path I'm on goes through those guys." He walked toward the exit and his posture changed from casual to determined with each step.

"Dammit." She looked at Zeb, who gave her a small head shake. *Yeah, I know it's not my fight. But I didn't read any dishonesty. So, unless he's deceiving himself, he has valid reasons.* She sighed, jogged to the bar, and spun her empty serving tray through the air to land in Zeb's waiting hands. Cali yanked the door open and slipped through. Although the street was empty, sounds emanated from the alley that bordered it to the left, so she headed in that direction and looked around the corner.

The stranger stood in the mouth of the corridor, his hands in the pockets of his jacket, and the others faced him in a rough semicircle. The passage was narrow enough to prevent his enemies from attacking all at once with fists but if they had magic, that advantage would be lost. She'd arrived as the leader of the four had finished talking but hadn't made out what he'd said.

The man she was concerned for sounded exasperated. "Look, this is a really simple question. Who's your boss? That's what I need to find out. You're in the clear. It's only a name."

One of the subordinates sneered. "We're not telling you anything, convict." The leader laughed, apparently at the stranger's reaction. "Oh yeah, we know about you, jailbird. We heard your brain is mush. Now, we'll have to show you what happens to people who mess with us."

Their opponent shrugged and his hands emerged from his pockets. She saw the slight flex in the back of his knees and the shuffle that reset his balance. The leader nodded, and the slimy one who had spoken rushed forward and a glitter of steel appeared in his hand. The man didn't move until the last minute when he shot his right hand out in a fast punch aimed at his attacker's wrist. A crunching sound echoed from the walls when his knuckles snapped the bone. The knife clattered on the asphalt and its wielder backpedaled, cradling his damaged limb.

"We don't have to—" Attacks from the other three cut his words off. The biggest one slid in with a boxer's grace and landed two rapid jabs to the man's chest that thrust him back. That put the giant thug in the way of the magic the fourth member of the group launched, a force blast that shoved him stumbling into the wall of the alley.

Cali rolled her eyes. *Nice coordination, fellas.* While it was likely the defender could handle this group, uneven odds irked her. Three on two seemed far fairer than three on one. She stepped around the corner and threw a punch in the air. A force fist pounded into the stomach of the one who'd inadvertently targeted his own ally. He doubled over and crumpled in a protective curl. *Damn. I gotta remember I'm stronger than I was.* Before, she could rely on her magic to be powerful enough to damage someone but not enough to really injure them. Now, her simple effort at distraction had taken him out of the fight. And instead of feeling subtly drained, power surged through her, promising pleasure and might if she'd let it off the leash.

Her partner had locked his sights on the enemy leader and used a sudden wind to lift objects from the alley floor and hurl them as he closed the distance separating them. Whatever attack his opponent had planned evaporated in the need to defend himself, which he did by bobbing, weaving, and occasionally summoning and throwing what looked like spheres of force magic to divert incoming projectiles off target. He held his own against the barrage until the moment the stranger's forehead came down on his nose. For a second, he staggered, then fell on his rear end with his legs spread and eyes unfocused.

The man with the broken wrist had vanished, so only a single enemy remained active. The big man shuffled in toward her without even raising his guard. Another force fist would finish him, but the magic inside her wanted it too much so she waited. When he threw a disrespectfully slow left hook, she quick-stepped away, guided it past her with her right hand on his elbow, and caught his wrist with her left hand. She slipped her arm under his elbow to hyperextend it and used it as a lever to throw him in the direction in which she faced. He landed hard on his back beside her partner, who looked down and growled, "Run if you want to live."

All three tried to rise, but the man pushed the enemy leader down again. "No, no, not you. We need to talk. I have a question for you."

Cali pushed through the beaded curtain, took a seat across from the man, and handed him a hard cider. She carried a soft one for herself. He drank half of it in a long gulp and set it down with a satisfied sigh. "Thanks. I definitely needed that."

She sipped hers slowly. Most of her mind was focused

on containing the desire to use more magic. Fortunately, it was diminishing but unfortunately, it was doing so far less quickly than she'd prefer. "So. You don't like taking advice, clearly."

He laughed. "So some have said. I appreciate your help back there." She'd waited while he finished with the enemy leader and sent him fleeing with threats.

"You didn't do more damage than you needed to. I respect that."

"There was no point. It wouldn't have gotten me what I wanted."

"Which was?" She took another sip and watched his eyes for any sign of deception.

"The next piece of the puzzle." She gestured for him to continue, and he laughed. "This story only works if told from the beginning. Let's start there. Hi, I'm Tanyith."

She shook his extended hand, tasted cinnamon-laced vanilla that indicated he was playing a little but telling the truth. "Cali."

"Only Cali?"

"Only Tanyith? Or, should I say, only Tanyith the convict jailbird?"

He scowled and took another sip. "Fair enough. So, a couple of years ago, I was part of a group of like-minded Atlanteans here in New Orleans."

Cali shook her head and the barriers that appeared whenever something touched on the deaths of her parents snapped into place. "A gang, you mean."

"Not in the same way that those idiots are in a gang." He shrugged. "More like a club, or maybe even a team. Fair enough, we crossed legal lines here and there but never with violence and never to exploit those weaker than us. We punched up, not down."

She stared and wished she had a reason to touch him again to assess the truth of his words. Doing it now would send entirely the wrong signals unless she admitted the purpose for it, which she wasn't about to do. "So you say."

Tanyith nodded. "Anyway, there were some who wanted to go in another direction and be more like the movies. La Cosa Nostra, but for NOLA."

"You were a few decades too late to take that role from what the legends say." The Matrangas were already part of the city's history a century before she was born.

He shrugged. "The ones who supported that plan weren't exactly the intellectual elite." His laugh sounded self-deprecating. "Although maybe I'm not either. My arguing against it earned me a one-way ticket to Trevilsom."

His breath skipped as her eyes widened. "Holy beignets, Batman. Are you serious?"

"Yeah." He nodded with a grin and drained his glass. "I was sure I was done for. But I somehow managed to preserve my sanity, possibly because I kept a singular focus on trying to find out who put me there and why."

"And that's what led you to those idiots?"

"Yep. I trailed them from The Shark Nightclub, which seems to be their headquarters."

Her eyes narrowed. *There are too many coincidences for one night.* "That's an interesting story, mysterious stranger." She rose. "I'm gonna have to ask you to leave now, though."

He complied slowly, confusion on his face. "Okay, sure."

She led him to the front of the tavern, where only a few

patrons remained and steadfastly ignored the stated closing time. On her way, she smacked a couple gently. "Get out of here, you crusty barnacles." They laughed and the normality of it made her grin. When they reached the bar, she said, "Zeb, this is Tanyith. He was just leaving."

The dwarf grinned. "Come back soon, Tanyith."

Cali shook her head. "Give it a day or two, though. We'd like to keep the peace undisturbed for a while." *And I need to check you out.*

A part of her thought he might protest but he simply nodded at her and waved to the bartender as he left. She leaned on the polished wood that separated them and said, "Zeb, that guy was in a gang here when my parents were killed."

His mustache curled downward. "There's no saying he was involved, Caliste. You can't assume it."

"I'm not. But I can't ignore it, either."

The dwarf turned to look at the now-closed door. "That's the smart choice, I think. There's definitely more to him than we know."

CHAPTER TWELVE

Cali peered through the small gap in the curtain reflected in the carefully positioned mirror. Emalia had a tourist couple in the two chairs across the table from her and used runes to tell their fortunes. She'd explained to the man and woman that their auras made the heavy etched stones the only appropriate choice to truly divine what fate had in store for them.

Bored with waiting, she yawned and stretched. The adventures of the night before had delayed her sleep for a few more hours than she would have preferred, given an option. At her feet, the Draksa yawned, looked accusingly at her, and put his head back on his paws. She'd been shocked when Fyre had blocked her efforts to leave her room. It took ten minutes of frustrating communication to elicit the knowledge that he wanted to come along. She'd invested another ten to explain that the woman who owned the boarding house mustn't know she had a pet and that he couldn't simply walk down the street in New Orleans.

He'd responded by leaping through the room's open window. She had panicked but watched him glide gently into the small backyard. Minutes later, she'd rushed down the stairs and out the back door in time to catch his shimmering transformation from a medium-sized dragon lizard into a large dog that most resembled a boxer. With a shake of her head and a cautioning finger pointed at him, she'd admonished, "Fine, but you'd better behave." His doggy grin was as effective at conveying his amusement at her as the Draksa one had been. A quick stop was made to purchase a leash and a collar to obey the letter of the New Orleans leash law and the two were on their way to visit the fortune teller's shop.

Emalia's deep dramatic voice informed the woman that she was looking for something, which was always a good grifter technique. *Everyone is looking for something*. What set her guardian apart was that, most of the time, she was accurate in identifying the object and telling the customer where to find it. Whenever Cali tried to discover how she did it, her mentor merely changed the subject with a small smile. To the man, she gave advice on how to position himself for a promotion at his workplace. The two left happy.

"They were nice people," she said as she pushed through the curtain and closed it carefully behind her.

"They seemed so. Did the runes work?"

"Of course. I never err in my choice of tools." Emalia filled a teapot from the electric kettle Cali had started, set the tray at the small table, and took a seat opposite her. "So, are you ready to train?"

She shook her head. "In a while. I have some questions first." The older woman raised a hand in invitation. "Okay, so...before, it always felt like I was drawing from a finite pool of power. Now, it seems like I'm full of magic—so much that it's trying to push its way out."

Her mentor delayed responding by checking to be sure that her long grey hair was properly restrained—it was—and by fussing with the teapot. Finally, she replied, "I can think of two possible causes. It may be a reaction to having your power suppressed. The pendulum swinging the other way." Cali nodded. *That makes sense.* "Or it might be that you contain so much power that you'll need to work extra hard to keep it in check. Your mother was strong and her mother before her."

She tilted her head. "Do you know my family all the way back?"

The woman lifted the pot and poured the tea. Notes of matcha and passion fruit filled the air above the cup as she placed it in front of Cali. "I do not. That is something you'll need to discover on your own if you choose to."

"Okay. So, how will I figure out which reason it is?"

Emalia shrugged. "If the pendulum swings back, you should notice. If it does not, you'll know."

The boxer at her feet snorted and she poked him with a foot. "No one likes a cynic, Fyre. So, okay, next question. Did I get any additional powers when my magic was unlocked?"

Laughter filled the room. "Of course not. It doesn't work that way. If you want to do new things, you'll have to study like everyone else."

Cali rolled her eyes. "Awesome. So, to sum up, more power, more problems, more work."

Her teacher raised a perfectly groomed eyebrow. "Of course. That's always how it is for honest folk."

She sighed. *Just once, would a shortcut be so awful?* "Then I guess we better get to it."

Her guardian hadn't been willing to close the shop for the afternoon to train her directly, so Cali sat in the lotus position in the small dressing area and stared at a flickering beeswax candle that spread suggestions of honey through the room. "The first step toward using your new strength is understanding it," Emalia had instructed. "Focus inward and find the paths."

It was an exercise she'd done many times before in order to allow her reduced magical power to flow without obstruction when she called upon it. She'd always been able to see the map hovering in front of her, lines snaking from her core, through the chakras, and spreading all over her body. Now, though, it stubbornly refused to appear.

Fyre nudged her with his snout, and she scratched his head absently. When her fingers touched him, magic flowed between them and the image she'd been seeking materialized before her. She glanced at him but he ignored her aside from luxuriating in the attention. "Huh. You're full of surprises, aren't you?"

Magic pulsed in streams that looked like arteries, veins, and capillaries. Cali focused on her illusion power and a set of currents brightened. She marshaled force, and another group gained strength. *Okay, I get it. More to draw from, distributed for faster response. Sure. That makes sense.*

She closed her eyes and pulled the idea of cold into her mind—frost, snow, and the way the shower hurt when the hot water ran out. Then, she envisioned the mist that the Draksa had ejected at her on the night they'd met. Her mind focused and investigated it, watched it stream past as she slipped into the gaps between the crystalline motes, and let it suffuse her. Without letting her attention falter, she raised a hand, seeking within for the paths that would bring the ice into her waiting palm. She felt a stirring and opened her eyes with a smile.

Her hand was empty.

"Damn it!" She blew out an annoyed breath. "Okay, that's enough for now." She rose and descended the stairs with Fyre plodding along behind. Emalia was in the back room sipping tea that smelled as if it had received a liberal dose of bourbon. The woman didn't quite smirk as she asked, "How did it go?"

Cali fell heavily into the chair across from her. "Great. So. Awesome." Her guardian laughed. "I thought of another question, though. What do you know about the gangs around here?"

A nod of the grey-topped head was encouraging. "I wondered when you would think to ask. Not too much. Long ago, there were as many magical gangs as there were immigrant families. But most of them departed for New Atlantis when it was completed. The last decade or so, there's only been one."

That lines up so far. "What do you know about that one?"

She shrugged. "For a time, it seemed to be an acceptable

thing. Now it doesn't. I've heard rumbles about unsavory practices and other noises about pressure on businesses. No one's come here yet."

The young woman laughed. "As if anyone could intimidate you into anything."

"True enough. And now that I have you and your Draksa, it's even less likely."

"As long as no one who has a problem with me decides to take an interest in you."

"You've been trouble since day one, child. I'm not concerned about it now."

Fyre growled as if to confirm he wasn't worried either. Cali checked her watch and sighed. "It's time to take this beast home and get to the tavern."

Emalia grinned. "Are you not ready to share him with Zeb?"

She shook her head. "He might think that a dwarf-snack would be tasty." The faux-dog looked at her with something that resembled a scowl. "What? As soon as I have time for twenty questions, we can discuss it." She tugged gently on the leash and he climbed to his feet when she did.

The older woman wrapped her in a hug, then stepped back. "Take care of each other."

Cali nodded. "Will do. Same time tomorrow?"

"I'm always here, you know that." Her mentor smiled. "And you both are always welcome, whether I'm present or not."

They walked out into the heat and only then did it occur to her that she had to think of a way to sneak the Draksa back to her room. She sighed and shook her head at him. "You're one challenge after the next. You'd better be good at sneaking because I can veil you, but I can't keep someone from stepping on you."

He opened his mouth only enough to stick his tongue out at her.

CHAPTER THIRTEEN

The training and work shift the day before had tired Cali out, and she'd slept in until almost the last minute. A rushed shower and a dash across the quarter got her to the station only five minutes after the time the Detective had named. She wiped the sweat from her forehead, took a deep breath, and pulled the doors open.

The building was old and well-kept, especially given the constant activity that required policing in the streets that surrounded it. She walked through a metal detector without setting it off, her first clear victory of the afternoon. A bored older man in a uniform grunted when she asked for Detective Barton and waved her toward a doorway in the rear wall. She threaded a path through the room and studiously ignored the open files and visible computer screens on the way lest someone decide to take a closer look at her.

Simply being here is more than close enough, thanks. She'd never had any issues with the law, and knowing she had the ace in the hole of being able to portal meant that if things went south to the level that she was imprisoned, she wouldn't stay confined against her will for long. But difficult as it was, she liked her life and had no interest in abandoning everything she'd built for an existence on the run. Plus, getting in trouble with the police wouldn't exactly be conducive to her plan to become an investigator.

The rooms through the rear doorway were small, clearly repurposed from some other use. Two desks arranged front-to-front were positioned inside the door of one, and Barton looked up and smiled. "Caliste. Thanks for coming."

She sighed. "Cali."

The detective nodded. "Kendra. Please, have a seat." She gestured toward a chair that sat at the side of her desk.

It squeaked as she lowered herself into it and for a moment, she thought it would collapse. *Old city, old station, young detective.* "Nice place you have here."

Barton laughed. "Yeah, sure. A real vacation location."

Cali's lips twitched into a smile. "It is for some, I imagine." Her server instincts rarely failed her and giving someone an opportunity to talk about themselves was one of the most reliable tactics.

A nod of agreement followed. "Any number of tourists find lodging here during their time in the city. But, generally, the folks out front go easy on them. That's not my area, and I'm definitely not interested in going easy on anyone."

"Tough woman in a man's world?"

She laughed again. "Nah. Merely a hardass who's devoted to her job. Which is why I wanted to have a chat with you."

On your own territory, sure. No accident there. She shrugged. "Well, here I am, as requested."

The officer's dark hair fell in her face as she looked at the folder on the desk in front of her, and she flicked it out of the way with a look of annoyance. "So, Jarten. How do you know him?"

Cali leaned forward and the chair creaked ominously again. "He's a frequent customer at the tavern. Usually on his own and occasionally with a lady friend of questionable taste." The other woman chuckled. "I never really put him in with a gang, though. That's what you do in the Specialized Investigations Division right?" She'd done some Internet searches between customers the night before to prepare for the encounter.

Barton nodded. "Correct. And he does seem to be hooked into the city's magical clan. Atlanteans." She felt the detective's eyes burning into hers, likely seeking any sign of a reaction to the revelation.

"There's many of them around, that's true."

"In your tavern?"

She shook her head. "No more than anyone else. Zeb has a very specific policy. Everyone gets along or they aren't welcome anymore. One strike and you're out."

The woman's chair creaked, too, as she leaned back. "So, is Jarten out then? Is that why you chased him?"

Cali kept her face neutral. "Jarten's still allowed in."

"So why did you hit him?"

The questions came as no surprise and she merely laughed. "Who claims I did?"

The detective leaned forward to consult the folder again. "It says here that an eyewitness saw a girl with long red hair fighting four men who were later identified as being part of the Atlanteans."

Her stare was one of calculated bemusement. "Are you seriously telling me I'm spending my afternoon here based on being a redhead? You'd better get Gillian Anderson and Christina Hendricks in here right away."

"And the subject was at your workplace shortly before the incident."

"That seems thin, Detective."

She shrugged. "I've had thinner. It's not so much that I'm concerned with this particular event. It's part of a pattern, though, an increasing willingness to mix it up in public where innocents can wind up endangered. That's something I am concerned with."

Cali frowned at the revelation. *Not good.* "That makes sense. Still, I'm not sure why I'm here."

Barton sighed. "Okay, don't admit it was you. We both know the truth. But the real reason you're here is that I want to use you."

Now, her laugh was a little shocked. "That's bold, Kendra. Buy a girl a drink first."

The woman rewarded the joke with a thin smile. "I need you to keep an eye out at the tavern and let me know what you see. You're uniquely positioned to do it since it's an open location for everyone."

She leaned back, folded her arms, and ignored the chair's protests. "Why not ask Zeb?"

"I'm not convinced he's one of the good guys."

Cali scowled. "You'd best think again on that subject."

The detective tapped her fingers on the desk. "Your loyalty is clear. But what do you really know about him?"

It took effort but she managed not to snarl. "My parents liked him. That's all I need to know."

"Your parents, who were killed in a suspected gang attack."

Her resistance failed, and she bolted to her feet. "Listen, lady, I'm not sure who you think you are, but no one talks about my family or my friends like that."

Barton stood and met her gaze, her aggressive tone a mirrored response. "You don't have the whole picture. I suggest you sit down and get it. For your sake and for your boss's."

The magic burned for release and it took a conscious effort to push it down. Slowly—too slowly—logic reasserted itself. *This is not the time and not the place.* She took a deep breath and sat on the edge of the seat, her spine rigid. After a moment, she managed to unclench her teeth enough to push, "Fine, tell me," through them.

The officer looked satisfied and Cali resisted the surging desire to throw a force bolt at her chest and portal out of the station. "A couple of years ago, things started to change. For about six months, it was a mess out there. Several human gangs warred among themselves and the Atlanteans took potshots when an opportunity presented itself. It finally resulted in two main groups—the Atlanteans and the human faction left standing."

She sighed. "We're not as effective as we'd like to be, of course, but we've managed to keep a lid on things since then. It's probably mostly because the gangs were regrouping and solidifying their holdings. But now, it's like someone lit a match and the whole thing has fired up again. Territories are in flux, big time. Not a night goes by without some block changing hands. Your place is unlikely to remain untouched, either by those wanting to claim it or by the random violence these things bring."

Cali shook her head. "So you say. But it'll take more than threats to cause Zeb to give in, regardless of who makes them."

"Your response is an example of the problem. You act as if this is normal, like it's status quo. New leaders have taken over both groups, and they face the same challenge—do enough to justify their positions of power. And that has the potential to do serious damage to everyone. That's why I need you to be my early warning system. I'm not asking you to betray anyone. Merely to keep me informed if you see something worrisome."

Despite her desire to reject the woman outright for being such a pushy jerk, she forced herself to consider the situation from an outside perspective. She sighed. "I'm not promising to work with you. I'll decide in the moment. But this will be a two-way flow of information or it won't happen at all. For anything I give you, you'll have to share what you know about that bigger picture you want me to focus on."

Barton nodded. "Sure. Fair is fair. But you can't bring me junk and expect gold."

"Deal." She stood more slowly this time and extended a hand, and the detective rose and gripped it. The banana flavor of suspicion hit her tongue, which was certainly expected from someone in her job, but also the faint hint of pineapple that suggested goodwill. She released the other woman's hand. "See you around, Detective Barton."

"Anytime, Caliste."

She wandered the streets for an hour while she tried to put the pieces together and failed utterly. Her steps had delivered her to the Dragons, and she pushed through the door with a resigned sigh. *Even on my day off, I wind up at work.*

CHAPTER FOURTEEN

Tanyith had put the information the fight had gained him into almost immediate use. After a much-needed eight hours of sleep, he'd followed up on the name the crew leader had provided. It had taken half a day of dropping the name among shopkeepers in the quarter before anyone gave him anything. Since then, he'd been on the woman's trail. More focused questioning into the late night and early morning had given him the location of a restaurant and a description of her.

That was why he was seated at a bar with a beer at his right hand and a plate of spicy barbecued oysters in front of him, his second round of each. Like many Atlanteans, he had a preference for products of the seas, but he wasn't a purist about their preparation. Some were, and in his experience, they tended to be more concerned about purity in all areas than he was. To him, part-Atlantean was Atlantean. To them, anything other than a direct descent on both sides was a flaw.

There were sounds of welcome through the restaurant

entrance behind him and to the right. Without breaking the pattern he'd established—eat one, sigh with pleasure, and chase it with a gulp of the strong brew—he flicked his gaze away from the Saints news site on his phone to the mirror that was the back wall of the bar. The new arrival matched the description he'd been given perfectly—pale skin and straight ebony hair that fell naturally to the middle of her back. She wore a sharp navy-blue business suit with a black blouse and matching heels. His quick survey couldn't capture the details of her face, but she exuded a sense of professional competence.

She wouldn't look out of place in a boardroom, and yet she's a mid-level leader in a street gang. Things really did change while I was inside. In his day, the Atlanteans took pride in rejecting the styles of the human gangs in the city. Apparently, that was no longer the case. The woman, Danna Cudon, was led to a seat alone at a table with a reserved sign. Two mismatched men sat at the next one over a moment later. One was very pale, tall, and muscular, and looked uncomfortable in his own suit. The other was dark, thin, and perfectly at home in a masculine version of his boss' outfit.

Tanyith ordered another round of food but switched to water now that his quarry was in sight. She selected the raw plate, and his brain automatically ascribed the definition of purist. While internally acknowledging that it was by no means sure, he wasn't able to discount the possibility either. Fortunately, her meal didn't take long as after the third helping, he really couldn't face a fourth. He paid his tab as her coffee arrived and headed out the door to find a vantage point.

He tucked himself into the shade of the doorway of a closed bar that would doubtless be under different management within the month, that being how New Orleans worked. His quarry stepped out and slipped her sunglasses on, reminding him of a celebrity. The men emerged and did the same, the perfect image of bodyguards, which was no doubt exactly what they were. He had the sense she would probably be adequate to any challenge on her own. Experienced practitioners could usually recognize others.

A black car pulled up to the curb, and he cursed as the trio slid inside. He looked around for a taxi but none were in sight. His phone wasn't set up with the apps to call for one yet, and there was no way a ride could get there in time, anyway. He jogged in the direction the car was headed and caught a glimpse of black rubber from an alley. A motorcycle was parked there, chained to a bar mounted on the wall. *Sorry, whoever you are. I'll bring it back full.* He made a yanking motion and the chain snapped where the bar tried to resist his magical pull. Tanyith directed a tiny burst of force into the keyhole and used it to turn the ignition and punched the starter switch. The bike roared to life.

He backed it out into the street and accelerated after the dark sedan. Pedestrians interfered with the flow of traffic, again merely a part of how things worked in New Orleans, and he was able to gain on his target. Within a few minutes, he realized where they were likely headed. The car turned into a garage about a block from the nightclub. Tanyith parked the bike around the corner and went back to watch on foot. He expected to see them emerge and cross over to it, but after ten minutes, decided that something else must have been at work. The building was a squat concrete bunker with only the rolling door visible. He circled it at a distance and identified another door but no windows. It was a mystery but now, he had two potential locations to investigate.

On his return to the bike, he noticed a flyer tacked to a telephone pole advertising live music at The Shark Nightclub for the next several nights. *So, a little of the old place remains,* he thought with a smile. *It's a perfect opportunity.* The grin faded. *There's no way I'll get into the club alone. They'll check everyone but no doubt give singles extra attention.* He considered asking Sienna, but there were abundant reasons not to, most especially the part where he'd put her in danger. He sighed. *I guess I don't have much of a choice, then.* Tanyith kicked the motorcycle into gear and headed back to return it where he'd borrowed it from before seeking out a partner in crime.

He managed not to slam the door as he entered the Drunken Dragons Tavern, which earned him a nod from the dwarf behind the bar. Zeb tilted his head toward where the cask rested and Tanyith held up a hand in negation. "I need my brain tonight, thanks."

The proprietor laughed. "A cider, then?"

"You read my mind." He slipped into the chair nearest the bartender and handed over a bill in exchange for the glass of amber liquid. His change appeared a moment later, and he drank deeply. His jaw ached slightly as the sour tang of the drink caught his taste buds. "Delicious." He leaned forward. "Can I ask you something that might offend you without getting whacked by the ax over there?"

Zeb chucked. "Probably. No promises."

"Your server. She's more than meets the eye, right?"

The chuckle became a heaving laugh. Finally, after almost a full minute, he raised a gnarled finger to wipe the tears from his eyes. "That is definitely one way to describe it. Yes, Cali is entirely unique."

Tanyith nodded. "You clearly find her trustworthy."

The dwarf turned serious. "Absolutely, I do. Not to overstep, but you're a little old for her."

He shook his head. "I'm not looking for a girlfriend, no worries on that account." He finished the drink and rapped his knuckles on the bar. "Thanks." He twisted and stood and quickly noticed her across the common room. She gave him a reserved smile as he strode directly toward her and he matched it and said, "Hey."

Cali raised an eyebrow. "Still not great at talking to girls, huh? Hey yourself."

He nodded at the alcove behind her. "Can you take five for a quick chat?"

"Sure." She shrugged. "If we hear screaming, though, I'll have to come out and see what's up."

He laughed. "Fair enough." He followed her into the room and sat across from her. "So, I saw you the other day outside the Shark Nightclub."

She stiffened. "Are you spying on me?"

"Spying yes. On you, no. I was watching the building."

While she relaxed slightly, her suspicion was clear. "Why?"

"I'm still trying to piece together what happened to land me in jail and how things have fallen out after, and I've hit a roadblock."

"That's plausible. Say more."

He shrugged. "They're having live music in there. I can't go in alone. That would make them suspicious, even if I was in disguise. So I need a partner. Ideally, one that casts better illusions than I do." He laughed. "Before my stint behind bars, I would have known ten people who met that description. Now, I only have one. You."

"What makes you think I fit the bill?"

"Your boss likes you and you can clearly handle yourself. I saw the precision of your portal spell."

She laughed. "Plus, you're desperate. And trust me, there are many people who don't like me." She paused and looked thoughtful. "But I'm already on their radar and they're on mine, so there's a unity of purpose between us." She leaned back and drummed her fingers on the table that separated them. "How do I know you won't kill me and leave me in an alley?"

"I've left a clear trail while coming to talk to you. Your boss could finger me and I'd be on my way back to Trevilsom."

"I'd still be dead."

"You're messing with me, aren't you?"

Her hair flopped in her face as she nodded vigorously. She emerged with a smile. "Yeah, it's kind of who I am. I thought you should know that upfront."

He rolled his eyes. "Perfect. So, you're in?"

Cali raised a finger. "We haven't talked compensation."

"What, you aren't willing to go in simply to find out what's going on?"

She shook her head. "Not as such. If you're going to take away my one night off a week to go see a band I probably won't like in a nightclub filled with people who might want to hurt me, I'll need a little more than that."

"Fair enough." He laughed. "Dinner beforehand?"

"You have yourself a deal. And if it's fancy, you'll have to supplement my wardrobe."

"That I can do. So, we're agreed?"

She rose and extended her hand. "Agreed." He shook it, and she smiled. "If you do turn out to be a killer, please don't dump my body in the swamp. That would be the grossest afterlife."

"Okay, I promise."

"You'd better or you'll find yourself haunted." She departed through the beads and immediately yelled at one of the customers. He leaned back with a grin. *Well, this gets more and more convoluted with each passing second. It's gonna be an interesting start to the weekend when Friday night arrives.*

CHAPTER FIFTEEN

Fyre and Cali were back at Emalia's before noon the next day. The Draksa had made it clear that she would not spend another afternoon away from him, and there had been no compelling reason to leave him behind. The walk was easier than usual, as people who wouldn't normally have gotten out of her way on the sidewalk gave the red-haired girl with the large boxer at her side a wide berth.

No fortunes were being predicted when they arrived, so they headed to the back room. Her guardian was waiting with the tea already brewed. Cali frowned. "That's some impressive timing."

The older woman smiled. "I told you, the teacher is attuned to the student. I felt your presence growing closer and assumed you were probably coming to see me, given that we need to continue your training."

She sat where she always did and drained her cup, then held it out for a refill. Since having her magic unlocked, the tea seemed more potent and cascaded like fire through her from the moment it touched her tongue. Emalia chuckled as she refilled it. "It seems as if you've come to terms with your new power quite well."

Cali shook her head. "Not really. I'm afraid to use it for anything other than defense in case I go overboard and wind up hurting someone. But that's not totally on point at the moment. I need more help with illusion."

Her teacher squinted. "Why that? Why now?"

She sighed. "It's tough to explain. There's this guy—"

Emalia interrupted with a laugh. "Ah, I see how it is."

"He's, like, at least a decade older than me. Please." She shook her head. "Anyway, he has issues with the same people who were taking a look at me. But he also has a plan to get inside and find some things out. The only problem is that they'll recognize us. So, I need to disguise both of us."

"He's not magical?"

"He's magical, but apparently not great at illusion." She shrugged. "He's been...away for a while, and it sounds like he's out of practice."

"Okay, then, illusion it will be. Your increased power should help here, but you'll have to be careful to contain it as well. If you wind up in close quarters, the fact that you're using magic might be noticeable."

Cali winced. "Close quarters are basically a guarantee. We're going to the Shark."

The other woman shook her head. "Caliste, that is a terrible idea."

"I know." She sighed. "But it's where all the trails lead to. I don't have any idea where else to look, and it sounds like he's convinced that any clues to take his investigation further are inside."

"Investigation? Is he a detective?"

She thought of how different he was from Barton and laughed. "No, although he clearly detects. I think he's only a guy who has questions that need answering before he can move on with...well, whatever it is he wants to move on with. He's kind of single-minded."

Emalia tapped a fingernail against the table, a sign that she was thinking. Finally, she shrugged. "If you are intent on this course of action, it is not my place to stop you. But you will definitely need a plan, a backup plan, and a backup plan for that one."

She smiled. "Which is why I'm here." Fyre barked. "Why we're here."

The older woman looked at the big dog laying on his side on her floor. "I don't suppose you're able to change into something small so you can be there to help?" He raised his head, thumped his tail once, and laid it down again.

Cali met her mentor's eyes. "I've decided that particular set of movements means 'maybe, but not interested in helping you right now.' I see it often."

Her mentor laughed and shook her head. "Ah, child, we all knew that you would be special. But none of us imagined how special. I hope and fear that you will always live in interesting times."

She finished off the liquid in her cup. "Well, Em, if anyone can teach me what I need to learn to get through them safely, it's you."

Taking the hint, her teacher ordered her to clear her

mind and focus on her magic. While she did so, the older woman bustled about to clear the table, lock the front door of her shop, and flip over the *back in an hour* sign. When she returned, Cali closed her eyes and pushed the rest of her concerns into their corners and secured them there. She opened them and nodded her readiness.

"You are getting faster at that," Emalia complimented her. "So. Illusion has two parts, each of which has two parts of its own. The first is to create the magic that will obscure your own features and the additional magic that will layer new ones on top. There's not enough time to teach you everything, so we'll focus only on faces. You will have to add appropriate physical disguises."

The girl nodded. "Okay, got it. Hide and replace." It was like what she'd done in the fight with Jarten's friends.

Emalia chanted softly, and her facial figures blurred until she looked like a mannequin. Then, new ones emerged to create a different shaped face several decades younger. She gasped at something that triggered a memory of her mother and realized for the first time that Emalia shared similar traits. "You're related. To my mother."

The older woman let the impersonation fade away, and Cali saw the similarities she'd missed for so long. "Yes. I was her aunt, although on her father's side." Like many ancient civilizations, Atlantis and New Atlantis traced the dominant family line through the mother. "We did not know each other well before we met here. But I grew to love her and your father very much. And you, of course."

Cali decided that was a can of worms that could stay closed for the moment. She imagined her features filling in and her face turning into a generic plastic version of herself. The symbols on her arms made their presence known with a slight shimmer. The second part, crafting a person, was harder. She pictured people she'd met, drew eyes from one, cheekbones from another, and nose and lips from a third. The symbols brightened, and her teacher—and great aunt—laughed. "You may want to select a single image and change it instead of what you've done. The result is rather…distracting." Fyre barked to add his support to the suggestion.

She felt the magic flow into her as the spell failed. "Damn. Okay. But I think I have that down well enough to practice. What's the other part?"

"You have to subtly convince others to accept it while hiding the fact that you're doing so."

"I understand the words you said, but when you string them together like that, it's like a different language."

Emalia laughed. "This is a magic you've never had occasion to learn. It'll take some time. Let's do a test first, though. Try to send a feeling to me."

"A feeling?"

"Yes. Any emotion. Make me experience it. Emotions are the easiest things to transmit."

Cali locked her mind on the concept of wonder and pictured the Draksa in his native form. She imagined the idea as a current in her body and pushed it toward her limbs, then outward. Her mentor smiled. "He is amazing, isn't he?"

A grin broke out over her face. "I did it?" A nod followed. "Fantastic! Okay, what's the next part?"

Her teacher laughed. "Now, you need to hide it so I don't know you're doing it. Take whatever method you used and make it smaller and almost transparent, scentless, flavorless—the closest thing to imperceptible as you can."

She did as instructed and after ten minutes of fiddling, had managed to accomplish enough to practice on her own. When she moved to rise, her teacher raised a hand. "You should be able to add something else with the aptitude you've shown. You're not tired, are you?"

Surprisingly, she realized that not only wasn't she tired, but she was actively energized like spending magic power had given her more. "I'm good."

Emalia nodded. "Okay. Now, in addition to the rest, you need to send out a cover. If someone does detect magic, you want to give them something to latch onto. Here's what I do." She didn't move but suddenly, the perfume she associated with the woman—a kind of a brittle vanilla scent—reached her nose.

"That's magic?"

"Yes. I haven't been able to actually buy it for years since it's Atlantean. So, I remember it with my magic. If someone notices, you have something harmless to attribute it to when you explain."

Damn. The old lady has some serious tricks. "Okay. I can handle that, I think."

Her mentor put a hand on her arm before she could stand, her gaze sharp and serious. "Do not take this lightly. You propose to walk into an enemy stronghold with only your magic to protect you. That might be fine if it were filled with humans—and let me stress the word might—but these are our people, born and raised with magic."

Cali passed on the opportunity to point out that she

hadn't been raised with magic. "I've got it. I'll be careful, and I'll keep working on it until I'm perfect."

She nodded. "Do that. And remember a backup plan."

"And another to back that one up. Absolutely. Now, Fyre and I need to go entertain some tourists. I'll choose something that lets me practice."

"Good girl," the older woman said with a smile.

They emerged into the sunlight moments later and sidestepped out of the way of a single woman heading in for a reading. She gave the boxer a pat as the customer closed the door behind her. "My great-aunt. How did I not realize that?" He snorted, and she scowled at him. "I don't know why I talk to you. I wonder if Dasante would take you to the pound for me."

His tail thump showed his complete lack of concern about her threat, and she sighed. *One of these days, someone will give me the respect I deserve.*

CHAPTER SIXTEEN

Cali had struggled through most of her shift without bringing the issue up with Zeb. He'd worked the bar, seemingly content with the evening, and doled out drinks and bowls of stew from the large pot in the corner warming oven. The tavern only offered one menu item per day, plus fresh bread from the bakery down the street, and the variety changed more or less on his whim. Today's was a spicy mix of venison and vegetables, which resulted in more drink sales than usual as the diners sweated through the food.

Finally, though, things slowed a little and she couldn't delay any longer. She delivered another collection of glasses for cleaning and wiped her forehead with a sleeve. "So, uh, I'll need tomorrow off, boss."

He gave her a death stare. "You're kidding."

She laughed. "No, I'm serious, and you're not fooling anyone with that scowl."

Zeb shrugged and returned to washing glasses, his

expression returning quickly to its normal serenity. "Okay. I'll see if Janice can come in."

Now it was her turn to scowl. On her days off, Janice was the replacement, although her main role was taking care of the place in the afternoon. She was annoying, overly flirty with the customers, and continuously angled to take Cali's nights as her own. *She'll love having to save the Dragons from my unprofessionalism, which is exactly how she'll describe it to Zeb.* But she'd given her word and besides, she needed to know what was going on with the gang. For her safety, the tavern's safety, and because it might have a connection to her parents, it was vital that she investigate.

"Be careful she doesn't get distracted by someone cute and forget she's working." She shook her head. *Petty, Cal. Petty.* "Anyway, it's important or I wouldn't do it. You know that."

He nodded and continued to wash and dry. "Whatcha got going on?"

For only a moment, she contemplated changing the subject. Her instincts always told her not to trust and she had to fight the battle to stay at least a little open every day. Then, she considered telling only part of the truth, that she had a date for dinner and dancing. But that, too, didn't feel right. So, she shrugged and said, "Tanyith has a lead on some Atlantean thing. I'll go with him to check it out."

He set the glass he was holding down on the counter that ran under the bar's top and asked, "Are you sure that's a good plan?"

Cali frowned. "You're not my father." They both laughed at her standard response to every effort he made to rein her in. "Seriously, it's probably not the best idea but not the worst either. I spent the day working on my illusion skills, and I have more practice time tomorrow after Aikido class. I'll be ready when the moment comes."

Behind her, the last patrons rose to leave. She walked over to say goodbye and collected their dishes. When the door closed after them, Zeb pointed at it. "Lock that, will you?"

She tilted her head in a question but did as he requested. When she returned, he gestured at Valerie. "You've never had the chance to see her, have you?"

"No."

He raised a palm, and the battleax flew from the wall to smack into it. After a single deft flip, he extended it for her to admire. The metal blades were unexpectedly thin but sacrificed no sharpness for it. Even the sight of it was threatening and the way he held it even more so. She lost herself in admiring it before he tilted his head up to the pegs that had supported the large weapon. A pair of etched ebony sticks rested there, previously invisible behind the ax.

Her palms itched. It must have shown in her expression because he chuckled. Another gesture brought them floating gently toward her and she snagged them. Each end was capped with black metal a shade darker than the wood. Dark scarlet engravings covered them in symbols she didn't recognize. They were gorgeous and felt perfect like they belonged in her hands. She spun them and flicked them out in a practice attack, and they cut through the air with an eerie whistle.

Cali looked at Zeb, tried to speak, and failed. She pulled her brain away from admiring the weapons and made another attempt. "They're fantastic. Why have you hidden them?"

He shrugged. "They're only sticks. Valerie is the real prize." His grin revealed the tease. "You weren't ready for them before but now, I'm not sure you can go without. They're yours."

"They're magic, aren't they?"

The black-bearded chin lowered in acknowledgment. "Yep. They aren't artifacts or anything like that, but they have a few tricks. See where they have an end with rings on them?" She lifted them and saw the markings. "Now, tap those ends together."

She obeyed and they snapped into alignment. With a glow, the seam between them vanished and transformed the sticks into a proper-sized jo staff. "Wicked." She spun it several times. The larger version was as perfectly balanced as the others had been but she noticed an odd sensation in her fingertips. "Zeb, why is it vibrating?"

He laughed. "It siphons magic from you so it can be ready for the next shape change. Don't worry, it doesn't take much."

"That's amazing. Where did you get it?"

That serene grin appeared again. "I know people who know people."

Cali rolled her eyes. "This is awesome, but I'm not sure why you're giving it to me tonight. It's not as if I can walk in with a pair of sticks or with a staff like Gandalf or something."

"We're getting there. Tell it to break with your magic." She frowned and parsed the instructions. She'd come to the conclusion, when discussing things magical with the dwarf, that his species' version worked differently than hers. But she put the idea of separation into her mind and pushed with her magic. The sticks obediently detached from one another.

He sounded pleased at her success. "Now, tell it to turn into bracelets that are the right size for you." She sighed, translated, and shoved the concept into the weapons. They diminished in her hands, retracted, and stretched until they were matching ebony bracelets. Each was wide enough to slip over her hands and covered about two inches of skin. Once over the bones, they shrunk to fit securely, immobile but not tight. They felt like they'd been missing before. Again, the sensation of magic being pulled into them was notable because of its unfamiliarity.

"How do I get them back to normal?"

"You have to be touching them but otherwise, simply tell them what you want." She called for the sticks, and the bracelets turned to a liquid that flowed over her hands before they returned to their natural form in her hands. "Holy cow."

Zeb nodded. "There is far more magic around you every day than you realize, Caliste. You'll discover it now that you're unlocked." He threw the battleax in the air and it curved with a flourish before it settled into its place above the bar.

She frowned at him. "You knew."

"Of course."

"When?"

"I figured it out a month after I hired you. There were power leaks that only someone who was around you as much as I am would have seen. But I was intrigued, so I did some research and found the right clues."

She put her hands on her hips and spoke in a flat tone. "But chose not to tell me."

He shrugged. "The way I saw it, someone went to great effort to limit you—someone you trusted enough to allow it to happen. It would have been completely inappropriate for me to undo that."

"But you let me go out and take care of troublemakers in your place, knowing that I was weak?"

The dwarf tapped his finger on the bar in time with his words. "Not weak. Never weak. You have always been more than adequate for any challenge. But I'll admit I thought letting you burn off a little magic now and then might help with the leakage. And might help you understand yourself better."

Cali sighed. "I feel much less bad about ditching work tomorrow, mister-secret-keeper."

He laughed. "Making you happy is indeed the main goal of my existence, so I am entirely pleased to hear it."

She stuck her tongue out at him. "Thanks for the sticks. I'll overlook the deception this time but next time, I'll let Fyre eat you. I'm fairly sure dwarf is a delicacy for his kind."

Zeb frowned. "Who or what is Fyre?"

"Ah, the all-knowing Zarden doesn't know everything." She laughed and waved as she headed to the exit. "What is the world coming to?" The closing door cut off his reply. *I'll pay for getting the last word in but damn, it was worth it.*

CHAPTER SEVENTEEN

When she stepped through the portal that connected her room at the boarding house to the basement of the Drunken Dragons Tavern, Cali quickly let it fall closed behind her. She didn't put it past Fyre to jump through, even though she'd repeatedly told him he needed to sit this one out. *Hell, for all I know, he turns into a bird and flies around the city while I'm away.* She looked forward to finding out more about the Draksa as soon as her suddenly outrageously busy life slowed for a day or two. At least she'd been able to practice at home so they could spend some time together. He'd seemed unimpressed with her illusion skills.

The portal had placed her in the corner farthest from the stairs, the only position not occupied by crates of supplies and fixtures. The wooden boxes had no labels, yet Zeb always knew exactly where to find what he was looking for. She'd decided it was some kind of bartender magic, probably the same kind that allowed a basement in New Orleans to be a useful space at all. Tanyith had arrived before her and was seated on one of them. He wore all black—shirt, tie, suit, and shoes. His hair wasn't in its usual pompadour and instead, hung down on the left side of his head. His beard was neatly combed. *It's already an effective disguise compared to the unpolished version.*

He patted a bag that rested beside him. "I brought you some going out clothes, as agreed."

Cali nodded. She'd worn her best dress in case, a black A-line that gathered around her ribs, but it was old and more appropriate for a funeral than a nightclub. "Let's get your illusion in place first. I need to practice keeping it there while I do other things."

"You're the expert."

She barked a laugh. "Yeah, sure. My teacher would be very amused to hear that." She stepped forward close enough to reach him. "This will feel a little weird." It always did for her, so she presumed the same would be true for him. She touched her index finger to his hair, and it changed color from a dirty blonde-brown to red. Satisfied, she made the same change to his eyebrows, mustache, and beard. "Okay, the easy part is over."

He nodded. "As long as I get it all back at the end."

"It might be you'll like the new version more. Although you do clean up better than I expected."

His lips twitched. "That's my first compliment in a year and a half. A little underwhelming, but thanks."

"Shut it." She concentrated until she felt the tingling in her fingertips and used them to redraw his face, changing his cheekbones and jaw to be squarer. It looked odd until she stroked his nose and shaped it to match. She stepped back and admired her work, then added the finishing touch, an octopus tattoo that began on his shoulder with tentacles expanding past the collar of his shirt onto his neck. It was a vibrant blue, and she included florescent touches that would glow under black light.

He checked the look in his phone and nodded. "Nice work. I definitely don't recognize that handsome dude."

She laughed and shook her head. "I'm not sure dude is the term you're looking for. It's kind of fourteen months ago." He raised an eyebrow as she took the bag from beside him and headed to a different corner of the room. "Now turn around. I don't want to screw up maintaining your illusion because I have to veil myself to change." He obeyed without a word, which she respected.

Quickly, she pulled items out of the bag and set them on a nearby crate top. First was a sequined shirt almost the identical color of her hair with hanging folds of fabric where sleeves should have been. Leather pants were next, and she noted with a frown that they were exactly her size. *That's very specific.* The shoes were open-toed with a moderately high heel, again in the proper dimensions. She called, "How did you know my sizes?"

"I found someone at the store who looked about your height and weight and told her to base them on herself but more muscular."

"That's a good lie but doesn't explain the shoes."

He chuckled. "You caught me. I stopped in and asked Zeb earlier today."

Cali kicked her fashionable pair of boots off and lifted the dress over her head, unable to resist the urge to peer over her shoulder and make sure he wasn't watching. He was still seated facing in the other direction. *Another point for you, mystery man.* She tugged and yanked at the leather pants until they were properly positioned and pulled the blouse on. Finally, she strapped the shoes on and used her phone's camera to review the results. *Not bad. And definitely not funeral wear.*

She stared into the lens and focused her magic. Her hair shifted from red to black and the curls lengthened into subtle waves. Her cheeks swelled slightly as she added a little weight to her face and softened her overall appearance. She created a tattoo of her own, a small blue and white wave behind her right ear. Her last touch was to veil her rings and turn the bracelets from black and scarlet to the same red as the blouse. When it was done, she sequestered the spells carefully in her mind to ensure that they would continue to work and power would continue to flow. Satisfied, she masked all of it to dampen the evidence of her magic at work.

Finally, she followed Emalia's advice and used her power to weave a citrus scent, fresh and clean. Tanyith sniffed and said "Nice."

She turned to face him and took a deep breath. "You can turn around now."

He complied and studied her for a moment. "You look older."

"Just what a woman likes to hear." She laughed. "Thanks, dude." But it was what she'd aimed for and it was good to know she'd succeeded. "So, where are you taking me for dinner?"

She'd peered through the windows of Galatoire's before but had never been inside. It was one of the most historic restaurants in the French Quarter, which was saying something. The white part of the tile floors matched the ceiling and the blue-green symbols that dotted it at intervals tied into the wallpaper that ran along the second story of the high room. Fans hung down on long poles from above, and the lights in their centers reflected from the white-framed mirrors that covered the side and back walls of the rectangular dining area.

The tables were close enough together to make the server inside her cringe, and she had to dodge several people before she slid into the red wooden chair Tanyith held out for her. She twisted and hung the thin strap attached to her small purse over one of the design curls on it. Moments later, the waiter arrived, tuxedo-clad with perfect posture. He aimed a glance of disapproval at her before he addressed her companion. "Drinks this evening, sir and ma'am?" Tanyith opted for water, and her request for Coke earned her a sniff of condescension. She resisted the pressing desire to trip him with a flick of magic as he departed.

Her companion's grin suggested he'd read her mind. She asked, "Are they always this snooty?"

He shrugged. "I've never been here. I always wanted to try it, but it wasn't exactly the right vibe for my particular group of friends."

"No girlfriends?"

His eyebrow raised and she rolled her eyes at him. "Listen, pal, even if there weren't like a decade between us, you're a little rugged and hairy for my tastes." He choked on the water he was sipping and she laughed. "Yeah, okay, I'm not really that shallow, but still. No offense."

He shook his head. "None taken. I was only teasing, but I'll admit that I might be somewhat out of practice at it."

"About fourteen months or so out of practice?"

"Exactly. So, to actually answer your question, I had a girlfriend a while back. Before you ask, more than fourteen months. We broke up because we had different world views. She was kind of like Zeb. Go with the flow. I'm…not."

Cali nodded. "Yeah, me neither. I try, but some things need accounting for."

He slapped his hand on the table hard enough to make the silverware jump but seemed not to notice the startled looks from those around them. He leaned forward and said in a low tone, "Exactly. The other way only works until something truly intolerable happens. Something that cries out for a reaction."

"For justice," she responded grimly. He recovered himself, nodded, and leaned back as the waiter returned. They placed their orders, duck and andouille gumbo plus crabmeat au gratin for her, and turtle soup and a pork chop for him. They managed small talk through the appetizers but moved into serious discussion as they worked on their entrees.

Tanyith led. "So, the goal for the evening has to be limited to getting a sense of the place. If we need a closer look, we can always go again next week. We can't afford to seem suspicious. At all costs, we definitely do not want to be noticed."

She glanced at her blouse, which reflected the lights

from above, then looked at him with a raised eyebrow. “Uh, are you listening to yourself?”

He laughed. “If it’s anything like I remember, you’ll be one of many shining stars once we’re inside. To be less fashionable is to be more notable among that crowd.”

“What are the chances that things have changed since your time, though?”

“Oh, probably a hundred percent. But I’ve been watching. Last night was the first of the shows, and our outfits are right in the middle of what I saw.”

Cali nodded. “Okay, well, if we have to run, I’ll trip you so they can’t catch me.”

“Fair enough.” His smile faded a little. “Once we get inside, there will probably be someone to seat us. If not, we’ll have to survey the space fast to make sure there aren’t any territories to invade.”

She tilted her head as she chewed and swallowed. “The crabmeat is to die for. Speaking of dying, what are you talking about? Territories?”

He stuck a fork onto her plate without asking and speared a piece of crab. “You’re right, that is delicious. So, you were in a high school once, right? You know how one area of the cafeteria is home to one clique and a different part is for another, and so on?”

“I get it.” She nodded. “Since it’s open to the public, there might be groups seated together and we don’t want any part of that.”

“Exactly. We’ll need to find the buffer zones.”

“Okay, once we’re seated, then what?”

He sliced a piece of meat free from the bone on his plate. “We watch. Soak it in. Enjoy the music. Keep an eye peeled for enemy magic. Hell, look out for enemies in general."

Cali shook her head. "That's really vague, Tee."

He looked startled. "Tay. My friends call me Tay."

She laughed. "I'm not sure we're friends yet. I'll stick with Tee for now."

He seemed about to argue the point, then shrugged it off. "We can't plan in the absence of information, so this effort is all about getting some. Focus on gathering every piece of data you can while we're there. Ideally, we'll see patterns emerge that we can follow up on."

"And if there aren't any?"

Tanyith sighed. "If this doesn't work, I'll have to do it the hard way. Find someone who has access and force them to share. I don't really like that option, though. It's dangerous and has the potential to go wrong a dozen different ways."

"So, you're kind of an indirect type of guy, is what you're saying."

His expression seemed a little disgruntled. "Has anyone ever told you that you have a real talent for being irritating?"

Cali laughed. "Once or twice, but usually in an appreciative way."

His flat, sarcastic tone conveyed the falsehood of his statement. "Consider my appreciation boundless."

She slapped him on the shoulder as she rose from her chair. "Wait until you really get to know me. You ain't seen nothin' yet. Dude."

CHAPTER EIGHTEEN

Their car dropped them off two blocks away from the nightclub. They'd agreed it would be better to leave their potential enemies no way to track them if things went awry. Cali was surprised at how comfortable the shoes Tanyith had selected for her were and planned to keep the outfit as payment for assisting him in the investigation. *And if that wasn't already his plan, he'll have to deal with it.*

They rounded the corner to find a short line of people waiting to enter The Shark, full of smiles and talking enthusiastically. It required a careful study to note that many had visible telltales of Atlantean ancestry—thicker than normal hair, skin that was a little healthier than the usual, and slightly larger eyes than the average. They were subtle but easily found when you looked for them. Of course, as her mother had said enough times that it was almost a mantra, "We see what we expect to see, regardless of what's actually there." Cali filed the information away to examine more carefully later.

When they arrived at the door, a burly man with dark skin and thick braids that hung over his shoulders to his chest stood in their path. He looked at them, his expression unreadable. "The cover's ten. Each." Tanyith pulled the required admission fee out of a money clip, plus an extra ten that he handed over with it. The guy nodded and moved aside to let them enter and pointed at a woman waiting within. She greeted them warmly. "Welcome to The Shark. Please come this way."

Her companion gestured for Cali to take the lead with a satisfied expression. The woman was easy to follow, her dress made of silver sequins over black fabric. The outfit sparkled in the dim lighting and her long blonde tresses and pale skin shone. The club's main room was almost exactly as he'd described it. A bar occupied the entire long wall to the right with three bartenders in white shirts, black vests, and red bow ties working behind it. On the opposite side was a small semicircular stage with three microphones around the front and a keyboard and drum kit in the back. A dance floor occupied the space immediately before the stage, and the rest of the room was filled with small round tables for two, some of them pushed together to accommodate larger groups.

The drinks menu on the table was several pages long, and there were a number of interesting-looking glasses being held by equally interesting-looking people around them. She leaned over under the guise of reading the offerings with him. "So, have you noticed anything useful?"

He turned the page. "I think we need to choose something fancy to keep our cover. Probably a Shark Tail would be best." He pointed at the description, which included rum, some kind of blue liquor, and a wedge of lime. She resisted the urge to smack him. "Order what you want."

"That's not what I was asking and you know it."

His reply was interrupted by the arrival of a waitress. She was in an outfit similar to the hostess, except it shimmered in blue. Cali received a smile, while Tanyith got a hand on the shoulder while she took his order. He turned to her as soon as the woman departed.

"Okay, here's how I see it. The place is divided into three zones. The seats over there on house left"—he snapped his gaze toward the wall the door was on—"are for members of human gangs. There's probably a plan to divide separate groups up, but I only see the main one here tonight. The Zatoras."

She flicked her gaze theatrically over his shoulder and he stopped talking as the woman arrived with their drinks. The menu hadn't mentioned that dry ice would spill mist over the edges but all in all, it was a pretty presentation. The server departed, and he continued. "Our seats are in the middle. A buffer between the gangs. House-right is for the Atlanteans."

Cali peered around the room and identified the divisions he described. The ones in the left area did seem similar in dress and attitude, while the ones in the right didn't match quite as well but had the "home turf" vibe. Those near their own seats were a mixture of locals and tourists. "Why do you think they're still doing shows and stuff if this is their base?"

Tanyith shrugged. "It could be anything. They want to be respected by the community or need a way to launder more cash. Maybe it's simply to keep the authorities a little less suspicious since a nightclub that doesn't have entertainment would be odd in this city."

She sipped her drink to avoid suspicion and winced at the bite. While she wasn't any more or less a stranger to alcohol than anyone else in her age group, she saw enough drunken stupidity at work that she had no desire to emulate it. Tanyith echoed her movement without the wince. She leaned in again. "I noticed the hostess heading through that door back there."

He didn't turn but nodded. "The restrooms are through and to the left if everything is the same as it used to be. Going straight takes you to the offices and probably stairs to the second level. Maybe a basement. I wouldn't know since I've never been down that hallway. Well, not when I could see anything, anyway."

"It seems like a good time to check it out then." She rose and patted him on the shoulder with some pressure when he tried to stop her. "I'm only going to powder my nose. I'll be right back." She snagged her purse from the table and headed toward the door. On the way, she gazed around like any person new to the place would and narrowly avoided crashing into a suited man who crossed her path. She muttered, "Excuse you," softly enough that he wouldn't hear it and continued.

The area behind the door was as Tanyith had described. The walls were black, the floor white tile, and an arrow indicating restrooms pointed to the left. A velvet rope sectioned off the corridor leading forward in case anyone failed to heed the *Staff Only* sign positioned immediately before it. She stepped into the ladies' room, stood in front of the long mirror, and extracted a lipstick from her purse.

The space was made claustrophobic by the babble of the others crowded into it busily adjusting their own looks. There was nothing interesting to hear, so she finished and wandered out again. A quick glance down the prohibited hallway almost caused her to collide with the hostess who was coming out of the main room.

Cali apologized, "Oh, I'm sorry. I was tempted by curiosity, I guess." She gestured at the area beyond the rope.

The other woman gave a short laugh. "Looking isn't a problem." Her tone suggested that anything more would be.

"Thanks," she replied and headed out into the club. The band was taking the stage to the sound of applause as she slid into the seat next to Tanyith. He looked over and asked, "So?"

"Nothing interesting. My look is still perfect, though. So is yours." She was pleased with the way the illusions were holding up. It required very little effort on her part since she'd stored it in a corner of her mind where it could work without her focusing directly on it. *Thank you yet again, Sensei Ikehara.* His reply was preempted by the arrival of the singer who belted out the opening lines of "I Put A Spell on You."

They relaxed and watched the show while they sipped their drinks slowly. Cali managed to accidentally-on-purpose spill a good portion of hers. There was a two-drink minimum, so replacements arrived without their involvement when their first ones were almost empty. They took turns surveying different areas of the club by unspoken agreement and one of them always kept an eye on the door to the restricted area.

She stiffened when the man who had trailed her emerged from that entrance to talk to the bartender. Her kick under the table caught Tanyith's attention, and he darted a glance in that direction as well. She whispered, "That's him."

He turned to face her. "I don't recognize him."

"Let's go and see what's in there. We're in illusion, so even if they throw us out, they won't know who we are. It's worth the risk." Her shadow slipped through the door, carrying two drinks.

Tanyith shook his head. "No. We wait, and we watch. No improvisation. It's too dangerous."

Cali ground her teeth in frustration. She wanted to do it. Her magic felt like it wanted her to do it. She'd never before been able to find any lead on her parents' deaths and now, one was in the same building with her. When she suddenly noticed the crowd was clapping around her, she realized she'd lost focus. She twisted to look at the stage, where the band was filing off, apparently taking a break. A heavy hand fell on her shoulder before she could renew her urging to Tanyith to head to the back. Her gaze rose to the bouncer who'd guarded the entrance and now loomed over her. *Dammit, we'll be thrown out. What did we do?*

She looked at Tanyith and saw her confusion mirrored on his face. The big man who stood between them rumbled, "The boss wants to talk to you two. Let's go."

CHAPTER NINETEEN

They stood at the same time and Cali watched her companion's eyes for some sign as to how he wanted to handle it. He gave her nothing, however, and simply maintained a neutral expression. *Fine. At least we'll get to see what's behind the curtain.* She followed her partner in the direction of the bouncer's gesture and toward the door that led deeper into the nightclub.

The man who she'd tracked to the club waited at the velvet rope, and he pulled it aside to allow them to pass. He exchanged words with the bouncer, who returned to the main room as their new escort gestured them forward and trailed behind them. They were about halfway down the hallway when a door that had been virtually invisible on the black wall opened on the left. A woman in a dark suit beckoned them inside, and she saw the back of Tanyith's neck tighten at the sight of her. *It seems like we both have friends in here. Awesome.*

The room beyond the door was elegant, completely at

odds with the club outside. It was covered with a lush brown carpet. The walls were a forest-green with art hung on each of them. Ornate chocolate leather couches faced each other across an empty space, with end tables at each side. They created a lane from the entrance to a desk near the room's far wall. Behind that desk was another woman in a suit very similar to her subordinate's. She was thin with tanned skin and deep-red hair that was braided and pulled back from her face. A dark shirt and tie were visible beneath her jacket. Cali pictured the matching trousers and imagined she'd wear sensible shoes.

She gestured at the chairs across from her and clasped her hands together on the polished mahogany top of the desk. File folders were stacked to her left and an expensive-looking fountain pen and ink bottle stood to her right but otherwise, the wide surface was bare. Her voice was smooth, and she spoke as if she selected each word with great care as she raised a manicured finger to point at Cali.

"You are the one using magic in my club. Stop now, or I'll ask Ms Cudon to make you do so." *Damn it to hell. I must not have concealed the magic as well as I'd thought. Kind of a big fail, there, Cali.* She considered denying it but decided being forced would probably involve a blow to the head. It was way too early in the situation to escalate things that far. With a sigh, she let the power fall, except the tiny amount that kept her bracelets' true nature obscured.

The woman nodded. "That's better. Thank you."

Tanyith replied, "Why did you bring us back here if you knew we were in disguise?"

The woman smiled. "I haven't reached this position by avoiding conflict, my friend, but by seeking it out. Why leave a problem for tomorrow when you can stamp it out today?"

Cali frowned. "That sounds kind of like a threat."

The club owner grinned. "Is that how you heard it? I really can't control how you interpret my words. Perhaps you need to be less suspicious. Then, you might not find yourself in situations like these in the first place." She swiveled her head to Tanyith. "I know you. Well, I know of you. I had just joined when you vanished."

He leaned forward and the woman from the door moved behind him instantly and pulled his shoulder back until he was seated normally again. The Atlantean leader smiled. "My people are highly concerned about my safety. Fanatical about it, even. You would be wise not to make any further sudden movements."

"So you're not responsible for sending me away?"

She shook her head. "Nope. Not I. It happened before I had the power to do it, not that I disagree with the concept. From what I've heard, you were a man of small vision."

He chuckled. "New boss, same as the old boss."

"Speaking of getting fooled…" She turned to face Cali. "Who are you, and why are you in my club?"

Tanyith interrupted. "I asked her to come. I assumed you'd be on the lookout for single men."

The woman stared at him and quiet menace crossed the distance between them. "If you speak out of turn again, Ms Cudon will break your jaw so you can't do so a third time. Nod if you understand."

His eyes widened but he obeyed. She turned away. "Answer the question, please."

Cali shrugged. "What he said. He needed a date for the

evening to make him seem like he wasn't alone. Plus, he claimed his illusion skills were pitiful but for all I know, he was sucking up."

She laughed. "But that's not all, is it?"

"No. I had my own reasons. One of your boys was following me."

"Did you wonder why?"

"Of course." She raised a hand slowly to push back her hair where it had slipped into her face. "But I assumed it was some street thug thing. Watching me to score some money."

The woman broke into laughter again. "Honey, we make more in an hour than you do in a month. We don't need your money. What's important is who you are and what role you might play in what is to come."

Cali's face screwed up in confusion. "What?"

Her partner slowly raised a hand. The leader turned toward him and rolled her eyes. "Is there something you need, Tanyith?"

He nodded. "How about we do away with the dancing around. You clearly possess information we'd like to have. There must be something you want from us or you would have thrown us out by now. Can we jump ahead to that? The kid has a curfew."

Her annoyed stare at him mirrored his partner's. She smoothed her tie and looked at Cali. "Is he always like this?"

"Annoying as hell? Yes. But he's smart, so I imagine that at least part of what he said is right."

She nodded. "Yeah. I do happen to have information

that you need. Both of you. But you'll have to do something for me to get it."

Cali summoned a car to take them to a big hotel on Poydras street, a couple of blocks off Canal, where they found a secluded seat in the restaurant. They both ordered coffee, and she requested cheesecake. The only conversation they'd had during the drive was her insistence that she deserved dessert for what he was putting her through, and his agreement that the demand seemed fair.

She leaned forward. "So, who is that woman?"

"The server? I don't know her." He had a half-smile on his face.

"Don't be a jerk. You know who I mean."

"All I've been able to discover are rumors, so I'm not sure. She's originally from New Atlantis and has gathered power aggressively since I was sent away. Her name is Usha, and it's usually said with some trepidation."

The food arrived, and as the server departed, Cali pointed at him. "Talk. Explain it again." When the Atlantean boss had laid it out, she'd used some kind of street jargon that resulted in several of the details sailing completely past her.

Tanyith took a drink of his coffee with a sigh. "Basically, it's a simple barter. We do something for her and we get what we want from her. It has to be both of us because that's the only way we each find our answers."

"I got that part. But what is it she wants us to actually do?"

He laughed and shook his head. "Nothing big. Only to steal something important for her."

She shrugged. "It seems simple. But by the look on your face, I think not so much?"

"You think right." He scratched the back of his neck. "The owners of the objects in question—a pair of derringer pistols that hearken back to the Matranga crime family—are the Zatoras."

She set her fork down with a clatter, her dessert only half-finished. Everyone knew about New Orleans' biggest crime syndicate. "That's harsh right there."

"That's how they work. They put you in a position of need and everything from then on only digs you in deeper. I don't know if it's even conscious. It's like breathing for them. Gang leaders are always good at that stuff. It's one of the reasons I'd be terrible at the job."

Her lips twisted in a wry grin. "Not smart enough? I get it."

"You really are a pain in the ass, you know that?" She stuck her tongue out at him and started eating again. "No, I'm definitely smart enough. But I don't have that particular killer instinct. Those people are individualists by default. I'm innately a team player."

"Did you say inmate-ly?"

Tanyith uttered a sigh. "I think I hate you."

Cali laughed. "No, you love me. Everyone does. I'll have to introduce you to Dasante sometime. He'll explain it."

"Boyfriend?"

"Friend who is a boy, sure."

He shook his head. "You never quit, do you?"

She nodded. "That's very true. I don't like it when bullies win. And that woman? She's a bully."

He sighed. "So, I'll at least look into it and see if I can find out what the hell her ultimate game is. The question is, do you want to continue? You could walk away now. While you wouldn't get whatever answer you're seeking, you'd be able to stay above all this nonsense."

"Why don't we both walk, then?"

"I can't because I need to know. I can't move on without the answer. I've spent days agonizing over it but without closure, I'll always be looking over my shoulder. It might have been personal and if it was, I'm still in danger."

Cali shrugged. "And I need to know why that jerkwad was watching me. She said it's because of who I am but I'm basically nobody. So, if someone thinks I'm someone I can't resist asking them why."

"You could probably find that information more safely."

"What would be the fun in that?"

His face registered confusion for a moment before he shook his head. "We're quite a pair, you and I."

"I told you, you're too old for me."

He looked like he would say something, then laughed. "If only your brain was as smart as your mouth, we might actually get somewhere."

She pointed her fork at him and spoke encouragingly. "Good one. Keep practicing. We'll make a funny person out of you yet. Maybe then, you'll be able to get a date with someone your own age. What are you, like, seventy? There's probably a Tindr for the elderly by now."

Tanyith stared at the ceiling with an expression she'd

seen before on both Zeb's and Emalia's faces, and she grinned. *You're gonna have to put in some serious practice before you're ready to word fight with me, Tee.*

CHAPTER TWENTY

Cali stifled a yawn as she rubbed the damp rag over a particularly resistant spot on the training mat. Her alarm had woken her up earlier than she would have preferred in order to have time to hang out with Fyre and still make it to the dojo early enough to get ready for the Saturday morning class. Worse, Dasante had apparently included a polka track on her random wake-up app. When she'd arrived, Sensei Ikehara had already been at the table he used as a desk in the front area when he wanted to be available for walk-ins. *I wonder if he has a secret Draksa that gets him up in the wee hours of the morning with demands for constant attention, too.*

Her ability to communicate with the dragon was improving, as near as she could tell. He'd appeared capable of understanding her from the start. It was the other direction that caused issues. Still, it seemed as if she was getting things quicker. He still laughed at her more or less constantly, but it felt like progress.

She hadn't been able to clear her mind as effectively as

usual, though. Even her old standby—imagining Mister Miyagi telling her to "wax on, wax off"—didn't get the job done. So many unknowns existed after the previous night's adventure at The Shark. She wasn't a fan of mysteries that involved her or those she loved, and these did both.

Frustrated, she pushed the cloth harder against the mat and let a little tension leak out. *There are too many damn puzzles. Every time I solve one, there's another waiting.* Tanyith's talk of not being able to move on until he found closure resonated deep inside her. Even though she had a plan for her life and was making good progress toward achieving it, each advance sometimes felt like a slog through quicksand determined to trap her in the present and never release her. Fortunately, most of the time, her head was on straight.

But not today. She blew a hair that had escaped her elastic out of her face and decided the part of the mat she'd been working on was as clean as it would get. The bell over the front door jangled as she lurched into a somersault and rose to her feet. Three men in suits stepped inside the small lobby, which was separated from the training area by a low wall with a gate in it. Ikehara stood but didn't offer his normal greeting. Instead, he stepped around the table. The first man turned to address him, but she couldn't make out the words.

The other two men stood a few steps away, one close to the front door and one closer to the mat. To her eyes, it looked like a defensive arrangement—two bodyguards watching over potential avenues of danger. She frowned and knelt to rub at an imaginary stain on the mat. In the moment that her back was to them, she whispered a spell, happy to note that only a couple of symbols on her arms appeared and faded quickly.

The magic was something she'd used often. Emalia had described it as creating a tunnel by shaping the air, which had proven a useful visualization. Now, that cylinder connected her ear to a position a foot away from the conversation happening between her teacher and the person who she suspected was a representative of the Zatoras. *Detective Barton was right. There's no staying out of this mess, no matter how hard I try. How hard anyone tries.*

Ikehara said, "I've told others from your organization this before, and I will tell you now. I am not interested in what you are offering."

The other man's tone sounded as if he was speaking to a particularly stupid child. *That won't win him points with Sensei.* "Perhaps you don't understand. Maybe you're not from around here. Let me make it clear. Unless you join our mutual protection circle, you'll find yourself defenseless when the Lants come for you. Now, that's not something you want, is it?"

She cringed at the use of the ethnic slur for Atlanteans. It wasn't something she heard often and never from anyone who knew her background. Her teacher replied, "I do not fear them. I do not fear you. I wish only to be left alone to run my business and instruct my students without interference."

The man in the suit laughed. "Well, of course you do. But that's not how things work nowadays. You have to choose a side or you'll find yourself crushed by circumstances. Our side has kept the peace for a long time in this town, not like those newcomers. We offer stability at a reasonable price."

Ikehara's voice was calm but firm. "Thank you, no."

The gangster sighed. "That's a very bad decision on your part. Very bad. I'll give you this one chance to reconsider at a ten percent increase to the cost for the insult."

"I am not with them. I am not with you. I am with myself. Your conflict does not interest me."

"The ant has no interest in the boot that squashes them, either. That doesn't make them any less dead."

She'd never heard her teacher exasperated before. It was a weary sound rather than an aggressive one—like he was frustrated over not being able to express himself in a way they could understand. She laughed inwardly. *Smack 'em with a bokken a few times. They'll get the idea.* The mental picture of the men fleeing from a bamboo sword put a grin on her face. Ikehara said calmly but forcefully, "This discussion is ended. The answer is no. Please leave. If I see you or any of your people again, I'll contact the police."

The three unwelcome men in suits laughed. "Oh, I'm certain that will help. We own the police, and the ones we don't, the Lants do. Good luck, ant. You'll need it."

In a movie, it would be the time when the gangsters would break things before leaving. She lowered her head and turned to watch in case they decided to attack her teacher. The minimalist trappings of the dojo denied them the first option, and they were apparently smart enough to avoid the second. They departed with more threats that Ikehara answered with nods and silence.

She let the spell fade and went back to her cleaning. When she'd encountered the gang by following the watcher, the whole thing had seemed like a low-stakes game. Now, she understood. It wasn't a game and the risks were much higher than they'd initially appeared. Her plans to spend the afternoon on schoolwork would have to wait. She needed to warn everyone she knew that the reality they'd grown accustomed to was no longer real.

CHAPTER TWENTY-ONE

Tanyith waited at a table on the patio at Cafe du Monde, sipped his coffee, and licked the sugar left by the beignets from his fingertips. He'd chosen the location on a whim and hadn't considered the reactions of others to the arrival of his guest.

She seemed well aware of how she affected them, though, and a smile grew on her face as her passage through the crowd toward him inspired whispers and involuntary flinches. Even in a metropolis like New Orleans, Drow were scarce. Nylotte's dark features and long ivory hair were immediately shocking, and the confidence in her stride seemed threatening to those who were easily intimidated. She wore black boots and black leather pants, with a t-shirt that hung off one shoulder and advertised a Nine Inch Nails tour from a decade before.

He grinned as she joined him at the table. "Did you choose that specifically?"

The woman nodded. "It seemed appropriate. Have you

seen Reznor around? Or Anne Rice? That's about my entire knowledge of this town, by the way."

"I don't run in the same crowds as famous authors and rock and roll stars, I'm afraid." He shook his head and looked toward the interior where the waitstaff were. "Coffee? Beignets?"

"No thanks. There are tasks awaiting me. What's so important that you believed it worth my time to come down here?"

"I need information, and all my contacts are either missing or compromised." He didn't think it was a good idea to get into the details of the gang situation. "So I thought you would be my best option. I don't want to have to sacrifice an organ to Chadrousse or anything, though."

She laughed, an unexpectedly happy sound given her overall demeanor. "Excellent, you do listen. I had my doubts."

He plastered a small grin on his face and pushed down the irritation that rose at her tone. *You need her. Be nice.* "Specifically, I need to know what's going on with New Atlantis."

That inspired a frown as she considered his words. "Interesting. I've had occasion to do some research on Atlanteans as part of assisting a student of mine. What's your interest beyond the obvious?"

Tanyith sighed. At some level, he'd hoped to get the information from her without having to share, but that had undeniably been a pipe dream from the start. The Dark Elf wasn't as obviously mercenary as the other man who'd helped to break him out, but that didn't mean she was uninterested in expanding her own knowledge and influence. "A gang of Atlanteans is throwing its weight around here. I used to be a part of it back when it didn't suck but now, it's full of scumbags. I'm wondering if there's an ongoing connection to the homeland."

Nylotte leaned back in her chair and looked around. A casual wave of her arm caused the surrounding sounds to grow softer. "It might be good to not be overheard talking about this. So, let's start with what you already know."

"New Atlantis is East of Florida and North of Haiti, in a deep trench." He shrugged. "I'm not sure where the original city was. Having never been to either, I can't say much about them. But there are more Atlantean immigrants in New Orleans than anywhere else."

She nodded. "And the gang?"

"It began as a way for those already here to help the newcomers. When I was part of it, we were non-violent and generally law-abiding, aside from a little gaming and some drinking."

"Anything else?"

"It's changed since then. And although there was some push for the kind of stuff they're doing now during my time, it seems like it transformed really quickly. The current leader wasn't even part of the group back then."

The Drow drummed her fingers on the table and leaned forward. "Okay. This might be connected to a larger picture. Over the last year or so, a group of power-grabbers on Oriceran have traded on the name of Rhazdon."

Tanyith's eyes widened. Everyone in the magical community was aware of the half-Atlantean rebel who had tried to seize power over the other planet decades before.

To hear him mentioned again out of the blue was shocking. "I thought he was dead."

Nylotte chuckled and shook her head. "First, Rhazdon is a she. Second, I think she is, this time. But really, who the hell knows with that one?"

"Okay. But how does that have anything to do with this?"

She made a gesture of uncertainty. "The group attracted a significant following. Maybe word got back to New Atlantis and someone decided they could capitalize on it."

"So what you're saying is that the gang's taking its orders from there?"

"That might be too cause-and-effect. If anything, perhaps they're getting support—people, treasure, strategic advice. Does that sound plausible with what you've seen?"

He ran the clues he'd already discovered through that filter. *Money from outside would explain how they've been able to expand so rapidly. The numbers could come from legitimate immigrants or ones sent for that purpose. There's no way to tell. But the last one seems likely. The boss didn't seem all that bright and could be a figurehead. And someone from the homeland would have both the broad view and the power to have me locked up in Trevilsom. It sounds right.*

Tanyith nodded. "That lines up reasonably well. It would explain a lot."

"So, what will you do about it all?"

"That's the question, isn't it? I guess the same thing I've planned all along, plus some extra. Find out who sent me away and deliver a proper thank you for my involuntary vacation. Learn how to block these jerks from taking over the city while also trying to make sure a gang war doesn't break out. Then I can focus on chipping away at the gang members and maybe get the group back to the way it used to be."

She raised an eyebrow. "With you in charge?"

He grinned. "Why not? I'm probably as useful a choice as anyone. But perhaps a group of leaders, instead of a single leader, would keep things on the right track better."

The Drow lowered her chin in acknowledgment. "That's a good plan. Most people who want power likely shouldn't be allowed to have it."

He could tell she was getting impatient with the discussion by the way her legs bounced. "One more thing before you go, if you don't mind. Do you have any idea who's in charge of New Atlantis?"

Her white hair swished as she shook her head. "I know it's been a hereditary monarchy at times and a republic at others. What it is now, I have no idea."

Tanyith growled his frustration. "Damn. It's not like we can simply wander past and find out, either."

Nylotte laughed as she rose. "First, there's no we here, only you. But you mentioned immigrants. Surely there are still some arriving now and again. It could be that you simply need to get to them before the gang does." She walked away and vanished quickly from sight as she headed down Decatur.

He shook his head at his own stupidity. *Of course that's what I should do. At some point, my brain will start to work again and then, this town will be in trouble.*

A shock of red hair across the street caught his attention and he stood hastily. He earned himself several outraged honks from those driving past when he darted across the road and he grinned when he confirmed it was Cali. She was playing a game of balloon volleyball in slow motion with a tall, dark-skinned man who looked to be about her age. A top hat rested on the ground in front of them, and he joined the small crowd of observers.

It didn't take long to conclude she used magic to control the flight of the balloon, which floated away from them. The crowd laughed. It was slapstick at half speed, and he found himself chuckling as well. When they finished, she turned and pronounced, "The amazing Dasante will return after a short break to astound you with feats of close-up magic and sleight of hand. Don't miss this once in a lifetime opportunity to see the ancient art of prestidigitation performed before your very eyes."

She smiled in recognition as he threw a dollar into the hat. Her greeting sounded happy as well. "Hey."

He laughed. *Apparently, this is a running gag now.* "Hey yourself. This is how you spend your free time?"

"Some of it."

"Nice control on the balloon."

"Always practicing, you know?" She grinned. "It's fun to get paid to improve your skills." She stepped closer. "Any fallout from the other night?"

Tanyith shook his head. "No, all good."

Cali's happy tone turned to a growl. "The Zatoras came to my teacher's dojo today and tried to shake him down. He kicked them out, of course."

That brought a scowl to his face. "They're really being aggressive. I don't know why, but it doesn't bode well for things to come."

"Which is why we need to get to the bottom of this

garbage and fast. Did you discover anything about the guns?"

He nodded. "They are definitely in the possession of the boss of the Zatoras. Anything we do will put us in hot water with them."

"Damn it to hell. These people suck."

"Right?" He chuckled. "We'll think of something. We still have four days before her deadline."

The man who'd busked with Cali slid up and stuck his hand out. "Dasante."

Tanyith gripped it and released it. "Tanyith."

"How do you know Cal?"

He laughed. "Oh, from around. Anyway, I need to head out. I hope you both have a profitable afternoon." He waved and wandered away, his brain ticking. *How do I turn this play back on the gang? There has to be a way.*

CHAPTER TWENTY-TWO

Cali pulled the laces of her sneakers tight and groaned as she rose from the ground. She glared at Fyre in his boxer disguise. "You owe me for this." The truth was that she'd come to really enjoy their early morning walks, which had lately become runs through the pre-dawn haze as she worked to keep up with him.

He gave her the look that suggested he was laughing at her—his mouth open and tongue lolling out the side—and bolted. The leash in her hand pulled her forward, and she stumbled until she stabilized her feet beneath her. Some days, she took the lead but since she had no particular place to go until work that night, the Draksa was in charge. The streetlights overhead were still lit, with sunrise some time away. Before the creature had adopted her, this wasn't an hour she'd seen with any regularity, and on those rare occasions when she had, it had been at the end of the day rather than the start.

They pelted through fancy neighborhoods and curved toward the quarter. It took a few blocks before she realized they were only a couple of turns away from the dojo. "Hey, Fyre, do you want to take a look at where I study Aikido? Is that why you brought us this way?"

He gave a bark that could have been a yes to either of her questions, so she guided him in the right direction. As they neared it, she imagined introducing him to Sensei Ikehara and smiled. The grin was wiped from her face when they came around the corner and she saw headlights turning into the alley alongside the dojo. She halted abruptly, forced her running partner to stop short, and knelt beside him. As she unclipped and dropped his leash, she whispered, "Something's happening up there. Sensei doesn't drive. I'm going to check it out. Keep yourself safe, okay?"

Fyre bumped her with his muzzle, and she took that as an affirmative. She focused her mind and changed her hair to blonde and her features to as close to a Barbie doll's as she could, then veiled herself for the approach. Even though the illusion would also muffle any sound she made, she was cautious as she advanced toward the alley. A wrong move in proximity to a magical could reveal her, and she had no idea what she'd discover.

She stuck her head around the corner and studied the five men and a beat-up van. They were all tanned, their jeans, t-shirts, and work boots visible in the spotlight shining down from above. One was directing the other four, who retrieved matching plastic canisters out of the back of the vehicle. They sloshed with the movement, and it didn't take a genius to conclude they were probably filled with gasoline. *I guess the Zatoras decided it was time to make an example of someone. Boy, did they choose the wrong place.*

She let the veil fade, stepped forward into the alley, and shouted, "Hey, fellas. How about you go away?" She cringed at the sound of her voice, which she hadn't disguised. *Stupid, Cal.* Most of her hoped they'd use the opportunity she'd given them to avoid any more trouble. The rest thought her commitment to giving them a chance to do so wasn't justice but stupidity.

The one closest to her—who had a really unattractive long mullet—swaggered in her direction. "Hey yourself, girl. How about you take your pretty little self on down the road? This doesn't concern you."

"So, we'll go with plan B, then." She smiled, targeted the one nearest the line of gasoline cans, and hurled a force blast at his stomach a second before she charged the man in front of her. He backpedaled but didn't panic as she'd hoped he would and merely set his feet and launched a strong punch at her face.

Cali ducked under the blow and continued her approach. Her magical attack had felled its target, but the other three had begun to react. One dove behind the protection of the van and another surged toward her. The third focused on the gasoline, which made him her next priority. She caught the flicker of metal in the fist of the one nearest her and willed her bracelets to transform. Her right-hand stick intercepted the blade on its way down and smacked it away from her body. She threw the left stick at the man who had almost reached the containers, and he flinched. It gave her time to punch the air and deliver a force blast to his chest that drove him into the wall. He collapsed. *Two down.*

She stuck her left hand out as she spun and her thrown

weapon returned to it but immediately froze. The two men ahead of her both held pistols. From behind the van, a voice called, "Okay, put the weapons down and you'll walk out of here alive. Maybe with two broken arms but still breathing."

Panting a little, she considered her options. The ones in front of her weren't the problem and a shield would take care of any incoming shots. But her shields were directional, and the third thug could hit her while she dealt with the first two. She looked toward where she thought he was and caught a blur at the top of her vision. The blue-green-yellow-and-orange streak matched the glowing symbols on her arms. She grinned and attacked the foes ahead of her.

As she moved, she threw both sticks and summoned a large curved shield with her right hand. The nearest man recoiled from the incoming projectile and his shots went wide and made loud metallic cracks as they struck the van. His partner kept his cool and fired four shots at her in two bursts of two. The bullets struck the curved force barrier and fell with a clatter. Cali drove the shield into the one who had missed. He had apparently also failed to realize that the woman with the snarl on her face also pushed a barrier of magic made physical in front of her. His nose broke, and he rebounded and fell.

Yelps emanated from behind her, followed by a scream that was quickly stilled. The last enemy standing emptied his gun at her but none of the bullets were able to penetrate her shield. She let it fall as he tried to change magazines and used a force blast to knock the pistol out of his hand. When she rotated her wrists to bring her palms up, the sticks settled in them with a solid smack. She held the weapons at her sides as she closed on the man, who seemed too shocked to run. The blood drained from his face suddenly and she grinned when Fyre stepped up beside her. His heavy tail swished audibly and ice crystals formed in the air with each breath.

She smiled at her foe. "So, I asked you to leave and instead, you thought it would be fun to attack me. The only reason I'll let you all survive this experience is so you can carry word back to your boss. This block and the ones on every side of it are off-limits. If I see you again, we will come for you one by one until you're all gone. Take your party somewhere else."

Cali raised her arms menacingly and summoned a fog that filled the alley. When she allowed it to clear, she and Fyre were already on the roof of the building he'd jumped from, watching carefully as the damaged hoodlums piled into their van. She patted the Draksa on the back. "Nice job of freezing that guy. I'm glad you didn't kill him."

His snout lowered. "He wasn't worth it."

Her head whipped around so fast she toppled to one knee. The Draksa stared at her with that damn grin on his face. "I'm sorry, what did you say?"

Fyre extended a claw and flicked a piece of dirt from his chest. "He. Wasn't. Worth. It." His voice was regal, slightly haughty, and definitely playful.

She frowned. "So, let me guess. You've been able to talk this whole time and have only been messing with me."

He nodded but didn't stop grooming himself.

"You know, you suck."

His laugh was a throaty sound but decidedly joyful. "I

couldn't help it. For what it's worth, it wasn't personal. I would have done it to anyone although it was much more fun than I thought it would be."

"I will have my revenge." She shook her head. "Accept this as truth."

The Draksa laughed again. "Threatening me won't work. I know where you live, remember? More importantly, I'm aware of how upset Mrs Jackson would be if she discovered you had a pet." He raised a paw, put it over his chest, and imitated the woman's high, screechy voice. "Caliste. You come out here right now and show me what's in that room."

They laughed together as the van pulled away. Cali shook her head. "It doesn't matter. I'll get back at you."

He grinned, his sharp teeth plainly visible. "Anytime. But for now, maybe we could find food? I'm starving."

So far, she'd bought him mainly andouille sausages for his meals, not knowing what else he might like. "What do you want?"

"A salad would be nice."

She frowned. "Really?"

"Of course not." He laughed at her again. "I'm a carnivore. Meat. Fish."

Cali groaned. "I think I dislike you. Can I take you back to the graveyard and leave you there?"

Her life partner uttered the happiest laugh she'd heard thus far. "No chance. We're stuck together. Trapped for all time. Or, at least, until you're sleeping and I eat you."

"Great, thanks for that visual."

He leapt down, used his wings to slow his descent, and shifted into dog form as he landed. She climbed down the fire escape and jumped the last few feet, then clipped the leash to his collar. Cali shook her head and chuckled. "You suck, you really do."

Fyre gave her a doggy grin and barked. She had no idea if he couldn't talk as a dog or if he was only screwing with her again. *Life used to be so simple. This is all Jarten's fault, and if I see him again, I'll have Fyre chew his leg off.* She sighed.

CHAPTER TWENTY-THREE

When she arrived for work that night, Cali told Zeb the whole story and he agreed she'd handled it well. He seemed preoccupied and moved about his tasks with efficiency but without his normal positive spirit. After a couple of hours, she couldn't take it anymore.

She set her tray down loudly on the bar and startled the nearest wizard, who inadvertently plunged the wand he was gesturing with into his drink. Carefully keeping the laughter off her face and out of her voice, she apologized and nodded at the dwarf, who handed over a rag from the stack that was always present at both ends of the bar. The hint of a smile hiding inside his copious facial hair eased her.

Once she'd mopped the spill, she stood on the foot rail and leaned over the wooden surface. "What is up with you tonight? You're like Superman, only instead of being made of steel, you're made of angst. Have you been listening to too much emo music again? I told you My Chemical Romance wouldn't do you any good."

He shook his head but couldn't hide his widening grin. "I have stuff on my mind is all. It happens sometimes. I'm sure you'll experience it someday."

"When my mind is big enough to hold more than one thought at a time, yeah, I heard it before," she finished for him with a smile of her own. Someone called her name from behind, and she raised a hand and yelled, "Shut it," at them without turning, to the laughter of the other customers.

The familiar creak of the entry door opening drew both their gazes to it and they sighed in unison. Zeb said, "Word travels fast. Best go do a round of the room since I assume you're the reason she's here."

Cali kept an ear on their conversation as she made her circuit of the customers while Detective Kendra Barton chatted amiably with Zeb. After fifteen minutes or so, she had things stable enough to return to the bar. In many ways, being the only server at the tavern was a nightly battle that required shifting strategies and tactics based upon the actions of an unpredictable opponent. Fortunately, there was goodwill on both sides otherwise, they'd have to add a second person which would severely diminish her income.

The dark-haired woman nodded as Cali arrived. "Caliste."

"Detective Barton. Always nice to see you. Would you prefer to sit in the common area or will you stay here at the bar? I recommend Zeb's cask selection." *Which will blow your too-smart skull off your shoulders for a while.*

Their visitor gave a thin smile. "Actually, I'm here to

talk to you. There was an incident earlier today that I'd like your perspective on."

She exchanged glances with Zeb, who tilted his head. "The small rooms are filled, so use the basement. It'll be quieter." She nodded and gestured for Barton to follow. The stairs were hidden behind the room's visible side wall and were both narrow and steep. She skipped down them with the ease of long experience and the other woman followed more slowly. After a moment's consideration of how evil she wanted to be, she warned the detective of the sudden low headroom at the bottom.

As she sat on the crate Tanyith had used a couple of nights before, she momentarily diverted into amazement over how much had happened since then. *Strong-armed by a gang boss, fought off pyromaniacs, learned that Fyre is a deceptive dragon who can talk. Busy weekend.* Barton studied the room as she walked through the small space. "It's not much of a basement."

Cali shrugged. "It's New Orleans. It's probably actually underwater." She'd asked, back when she'd been new at the job, and Zeb had simply replied, "Magic."

The detective chuckled. "Well, that makes me feel so much better about it. Thanks for that. So, do you know why I'm here?"

She put an innocent expression on her face and mimicked the vacant Barbie doll one she'd worn earlier. "I have no idea, officer. Parking tickets? Charity softball game sponsorship?"

Barton sighed and pinched the bridge of her nose. "You know, I've arrested people who were more helpful than you are."

"Take me away, officer." She held out her wrists. "I could use the rest."

The other woman chuckled darkly. "Yeah, that's why I'm here. Do you want to tell me what happened in the alley beside Ikehara Goro's place?"

"Sensei Ikehara," she corrected automatically like she always did when a potential customer asked for him by his full name. *I wonder where they're getting it, though. Maybe I should have a look at his website.* She put it at the end of her mental to-do list, which meant that at the current rate of accomplishment, it would probably be three and a half years before she got to it. *Longer, if Barton has her way.*

"So, what's the story?"

Cali shook her head. Zeb had agreed she shouldn't directly implicate herself if anyone ever asked. "Well, I did hear about something from my friends on the Square. I'm not sure where they got it from."

"I don't know what I disbelieve more—that you weren't involved or that you have friends."

"One point to the detective." She laughed and raised her index finger. "Anyway, my friends told me some firebugs who weren't in their right minds had gasoline and planned to use it on one of the buildings around there. I didn't hear which. Apparently, other people showed up and kicked their asses."

"Not people, person," Barton said crisply. "One. A woman from what my friends are saying."

"If you're as pushy with them as you are with me, they probably only tell you what you want to hear."

"Caliste..." She paused and seemed frustrated. "Look. I don't want to do this dance with you. We have a very real threat and you're in the middle of it. I don't know why, but I do know you've put yourself in danger and you'll put your boss in danger, and it's not a huge jump from there to find your grandmother or whatever in her psychic shop."

Cali's body stilled and the magic inside her signaled its readiness to fight. "Detective, threatening my family is not the way to get what you want."

The other woman shoved her hands in her leather jacket and started to pace. "I'm warning, not threatening. I have no reason to go after you or anyone you care about unless you give me one. But you're in a unique position and you seem to be digging yourself in deeper every day." She opened her mouth to protest and Barton talked over her. "Whatever. Please listen. I know you can do magic and there is zero doubt in my mind that it was you in the alley. The disguise was a good idea and it might trick them. It didn't fool the traffic cameras that spotted you headed in that direction. You have a nice-looking dog, by the way."

She heaved a sigh. "I won't confirm or deny, but those scumbags got much less than they deserved."

Barton nodded. "You'll have no argument from me. It's part of my job to keep gang stuff from spilling onto innocents, so whoever stopped them did me a favor. But magic doesn't make you a superhero these days, and criminal organizations have money to buy information on those who thwart them."

"Lucky we don't know anyone who does that."

The detective sighed and sat on a crate across from her. "Yeah, lucky. So, do you have anything that might be useful or did I waste my time coming here?"

Cali took a moment to think. *It all comes down to trust.*

Can I trust her? The voice of caution that always appeared at moments like this told her no, but she'd learned to filter its warnings through other lenses. "Okay, here's what I have. There are two big groups who've both apparently decided it's time to take on the other."

Her visitor nodded. "The Zatoras and the Atlanteans."

"Right. They're working the streets to extort protection, and loyalty, I guess?"

Barton shook her head. "It's less about loyalty than ownership. The people they exploit would turn on them in an instant if the boot on their necks got any lighter."

The image made her angry. "But I have it on good authority that they're escalating the battle. That direct attacks aren't far away."

A slow frown slid over the detective's expression. "That's bad. I presume your sources are reliable?"

"Without a doubt."

"Damn. And you're right in the middle of it all, I bet."

She shrugged. "I seem to attract trouble. I'm guessing pheromones."

"It's not something to joke about."

"Everything is something to joke about. Otherwise, I'd sit in my room all day overwhelmed by it all."

Barton rose again. "Do your people know they're in danger because of you?"

Ouch. "I'll make sure they're all on the lookout, Detective."

"I have one more question for you, and you should really think about answering it honestly. Do you have backup?"

She thought of Tanyith and his hipster pompadour, and

then of Fyre waiting for her at home. Of Zeb and Valerie and of Emalia and her own subtle magics. Warmth accompanied each remembrance. "Yeah, I do."

"Good. I have a feeling you'll need it. Now, one other thing. Do I get to meet your mystery man at some point?"

Cali blinked and failed to keep the surprise off her face, which made the other woman grin. "All those cameras, remember, and once we know who to look for, it's easy to track."

"I'm not sure I'm comfortable with that." She frowned.

The detective shrugged. "Whether or not it should exist is above my pay grade. But using it to avoid bloodshed on the streets? Yeah. I don't have a huge problem with that."

"And tracking me accomplishes that?"

"I didn't put you into this, Caliste. That was all you. If you'd wanted to stay off the radar, you could have simply let Jarten go."

Her lips twisted in a grin. "Jarten who?"

The other woman laughed. "Well, I'm glad we had this talk. You should consider letting me meet your backup, though. I have good instincts about people."

Cali rose and raised an arm to indicate the stairs. "As fun as this conversation has been, I should probably get back to work." She followed the detective up to the main floor, grabbed a tray, and headed over to take care of her charges. Her glance strayed to the bar as Barton said her goodbyes to Zeb and departed.

After the urgent needs were addressed, she found a moment to chat with the bartender. He still looked preoccupied. In fact, more so than before she'd headed to the basement with the detective. She frowned. "What's going on with you today?"

He shook his head. "I liked the city fine the way she was. The idiots trying to change her are too concerned with their own needs and fail to understand that they're part of a whole."

"They know they're part of a whole. It's only that their definition of who that includes is far smaller than ours."

"Yes. Which is a recipe for trouble." The dwarf shook his head. "You be careful. Don't let the man with the inferior beard get you hurt."

"No worries." She laughed. "I already told him I'll leave him behind at a moment's notice."

"Good girl." He grinned but it didn't reach his eyes. "See that you do."

She knew that he knew she wasn't capable of such a thing, but she nodded and smiled anyway. "Right on, boss."

CHAPTER TWENTY-FOUR

Zeb locked the door behind Cali and threw the extra bolts that would keep it secure against most humans. A Kilomea might get through but would regret doing so when the defensive wards reacted to the intrusion. Years of practice and exploration had taught him how to craft spells sensitive to the nature of an invader. This allowed him to use deterrents strong enough to affect a larger creature without worrying that they would accidentally kill a smaller one.

He invoked the tavern's normal defenses, which glowed in his sight as they came to life. As he always did, he traced them with his eyes to ensure that none had been broken or compromised. They were fine, as expected. A wave extinguished the lights and turned off the warming oven. He carried the heavy half-full pot of stew to the basement and set it down in the middle of the floor. With a two-handed gesture, he telekinetically lifted the crates piled against one wall and floated them out of the way to expose a bare brick surface.

Unhurried, he placed his hands on two particular protrusions and pushed his magic into them. The wall shifted inward and slid aside. Lights warmed slowly around the large rectangular room beyond as he carried the stew forward and hung it on a hook inside a stone fireplace. A flick of his fingers darted a fireball into the wood beneath, and the resulting blaze immediately started to banish the damp chill.

It took a great deal of magic to protect this hidden space from a variety of threats. First, from the elements that battered constantly against its boundaries. Second, from magical intrusions by those allies who knew of its existence. And third, from those enemies who might seek to discover it. A complex spell threaded through the walls of the common room above siphoned minuscule traces of arcane power from his patrons to keep the room's defenses active.

A round table dominated the center of the chamber, with a couple of feet of clearance all around except at the far end. That portion of the area, a square the width of the room, was reserved for portals. A shimmering barrier that only he knew how to lower enclosed it in all directions to ensure no one could get out of the landing area without his participation. A cupboard stood tall on the wall opposite the fireplace, and he used magic to move bowls, utensils, and cups from it to the places at the table.

It was large enough to fit ten comfortably but tonight, there were only seven chairs. The representative of the Atlantean gang had declined his invitation as she always did. It was likely for the best this evening, given that her organization, along with the human criminal group, would be the main topics of discussion.

The Light Elf was the first to arrive. Everything about him was pale, from his light hair to his suede boots. He was the newest member of the gathering, appointed after the previous designee made the decision to return to Oriceran. Zeb waited until his portal vanished, parted the barrier so his guest could step into the main part of the room, and snapped it into place again as soon as he cleared the boundary.

"Malonne. Thank you for coming."

The elf inclined his sharp chin. "Of course. It's a pleasure to be invited."

The dwarf pointed at four casks resting on a deep shelf on the room's entry wall, which had slid closed again. "Red wine, white wine, hard cider, and soft cider." His guest took a cup from the table and headed over. His host's attention was pulled away from watching his selection by the opening of the next portal.

Ten minutes later, everyone had arrived, filled cups and bowls, and taken their seats. The most senior of them, an elderly white-haired wizard who could often be found holding court in the common room above, nodded toward him. "I'd like to thank Zeb for hosting us, as always." The others murmured agreement to the formality.

He continued, "Our main topic of conversation today is, of course, the growing influences of the Zatora and Atlantean gangs in town. They have refused all entreaties to desist. As a collective, we must choose a path forward in the face of this escalating situation."

The rules of the group awarded speaking priority by circling the table clockwise. To the wizard's left was the Light Elf, who declined to speak. The witch beside him, a brunette in a Tulane sweatshirt and faded blue jeans gave her opinion in an unexpectedly raspy voice. "We should band together and wipe them both out. If they're not with us, we should get them out of our lives."

Zeb laughed, as did several others at the table. Delia was always one to pursue the aggressive path. It had long served her well, usually to the benefit of those who followed her. Those who survived the battles she started, anyway.

The Kilomean male who was next in line shook his giant head. Brukirot's people tended toward physical labor when in the city but spent the majority of their time in the swamps, surviving off the land. "While we shouldn't permit them to encroach on those areas we consider ours, as long as they are fighting over human territory, why should we care?"

Nods and head shakes were offered in response. It was a common question, and those on either side were generally unwilling to cross the line. Zeb took his turn and simply reminded the others that all their livelihoods were tied to those of the humans in the city, however much they might prefer to deny it.

Next was the Drow, Invel. He walked the boundary between legal and illegal activities with impressive grace and procured and sold items of questionable providence without concern for anything other than the profit to be made. His long straight hair was the color of cold ashes, and his skin was mottled with patches of light among the dark. Zeb suspected he'd faced discrimination from his own kind over that—or over something anyway—because he tended toward open-mindedness where the other species were concerned. His voice was the opposite of Delia's, smooth and unchallenging. "It seems to me that in the face of these bold moves, we can't remain neutral. We need to act to maintain stability." Unspoken but understood was the knowledge that his business flourished best when things were stable and predictable.

The last person at the table was a gnome. Scoppic was energetic and almost frenetic. His job required him to be quiet, as he was in charge of maintaining the collections and organizations for all the libraries in the city. Zeb often imagined that his constant motion at the gatherings was the yang to his occupation's yin. He bounced slightly in his chair and took a deep drink of his cider before he spoke. "We surely must take action of some kind. But to do so requires more information than we possess. We have to gather intelligence on them both. Is there any reason we might not have time to do that before deciding?"

The wizard, Vizidus, shrugged. "We have far more unknowns than knowns. I believe we must act to deter their expansion, but my friend here is right. We need to find out more, also. I suggest we do both. We can make small moves to corral the spread of their territories while seeking information to guide us in the question of greater involvement. Is this agreeable?"

There were grumbles, especially from Delia, but ultimately, everyone acquiesced to the plan. The conversation turned to other matters and after an hour, his guests departed, all save Invel, who was wont to stay and chat. Zeb liked the Drow personally and moreover appreciated his thoughtful stance on the various issues the group debated. The Dark Elf tended to view things in economic terms, but that was a useful perspective for many decisions. He limped slightly as he brought two mugs of hard cider back to the table and sat down beside Zeb with a sigh. "So, that went about as well as one could have expected."

The dwarf nodded and drank half the cup. "Agreed. Some people simply will never change."

"Do you think this situation can end without us all being drawn into the fight?"

Zeb shrugged. "Only if we choose to hide and let the humans deal with it on their own. And if we do that, which of us is next to be abandoned? The city will only be strong if we are prepared to come together. Talking about 'they' and 'them' doesn't make us safer or more stable."

Invel nodded and sighed into his drink. "It was easier before the human gangs consolidated and the Atlanteans changed."

He laughed. "Well, sure. But remember, chaos is invariably good for people like us, who provide specialized tools for protection and alcohol for celebration or regret."

"So declares the most peace-loving of us all."

"Always look on the bright side of life, isn't that what the movie says?"

The Drow groaned as he rose. "Fantastic. That's the earworm I needed to make my day complete." He tapped his feet together and made a small bow. "Until next time, my friend."

As he mounted the stage and portaled away, Zeb gave him a wave. Once he was gone, the dwarf sighed. "It'll get worse before it improves, I think," he announced to the empty room. "I guess I'd better make sure the wards are topped off."

CHAPTER TWENTY-FIVE

Now that Fyre had revealed his ability to speak, he wouldn't shut up. Cali growled irritably. "Would you let me think for a moment, please?" He had expounded on the fact that her apartment was really too small for them and they should spend more time out walking together.

After a half-hour of wandering, she faced a difficult decision as his nattering had caused her to lose track of time. She could either run home, drop him off, and dash to the dojo for her morning tasks, or bring him along and trust him to behave. They'd agreed she didn't need to see his dog illusion, so where others saw the boxer, she perceived the Draksa in his natural form. She stopped and stared at him. "Look, if I leave you tied up outside the door of the Aikido studio, can you hang out without causing trouble for a few hours? Otherwise, I'll have to take you home."

He nodded enthusiastically. "Can do, will do, happy to do, most definitely want to do."

She rolled her eyes. "You're deliberately trying to wreck my sanity, aren't you? Why would you be like this?"

His laugh was a strange sound but conveyed the idea of "laughing at" versus "laughing with" really effectively. He was doing the former at the moment but stopped and sat primly. "I would never, ever, do such a thing. You wound me."

I swear to heaven, he's a cat in a dragon's body. She shook her head and jogged toward the dojo.

Ikehara Goro was already there when she arrived, seemingly lost in thought as he walked a slow square around the mat. When the door swung shut behind her, he broke from his reverie and smiled. "Caliste, I have been waiting for you."

She looked at her watch. "Am I late?"

He shook his head. "No. As ever, you are on time. Please, come into my office."

Cali had never been in the small room at the back of the studio before. It was always closed and presumably locked, although she'd never tried it. Her tasks were clear and specifically did not involve that area. He opened the door and ushered her inside, where an exact copy of his front table filled most of the space and the metal chairs and file cabinets occupied the rest. In silence, he sat behind the open laptop that rested on the table and motioned her to the chair across from him.

"So, I have not asked too many questions about you

before, which makes this somewhat awkward. But I believe this was you. Am I correct?"

He spun the computer to reveal a high-angle view of her battle with the men in the van outside the dojo. Cold fear swept through her at the sight and the realization that someone she considered one of the rocks in her life might react badly to her actions. They watched the video in silence. When it paused at the end, she swallowed hard against the dryness in her throat. Lying wasn't an option, not to him. "Yes. It was me. How did you know?"

The sensei chuckled, spun the laptop into its original position, and lowered the lid. "We have trained together for some time. Did you think I wouldn't recognize the way you move and the way you fight? Even if I had doubts, how you used the sticks would have eliminated them."

She nodded. "I should have realized that. Although I didn't know you had a camera. Not that it would have made a difference."

He gave her a soft smile. "With the increasing pressure from all sides, a security system seemed a smart idea. However, it only comes to me and will be automatically deleted shortly—unless you'd like a copy."

Cali laughed and his joke eased her tension somewhat. "No, Sensei. I'm good, thanks."

"That's quite the partner you have." He raised an eyebrow. "And you are yourself skilled in magic if I followed the battle correctly."

"I'm learning. My teacher would say slowly but surely."

"The sticks—are they magical? Or do you simply use magic on them?"

"They have their own magic—transformation and the ability to return to my hand if I will them to."

He nodded as if he'd expected the answer. "May I see them?"

She wasn't capable of distrusting Ikehara so she stood, pushed the sleeves of her sweatshirt up to show the bracelets, and willed them to turn into weapons. They flowed over her hands and assumed their proper shape. His eyes widened at the sight but he didn't respond. She flipped the right one and held it out to him, then did the same with the left. He examined them closely and peered along each etched groove as if it had secrets to reveal.

After several moments, he shook his head. "These are beautiful and weighted perfectly. What are the rings for?"

Cali smiled. "Touch those ends together." He complied but nothing happened. She frowned. "Hmm. Maybe they don't have enough magic." She touched one with her finger. "Try again." Once more, the sticks refused to perform. "Huh. I guess when Zeb said they were mine, he really meant they were mine." She grasped them and pressed the ends together, and they snapped into place and became a single jo staff.

"Wonderful," Ikehara whispered and spun it carefully overhead. "Let's go out onto the mat." He returned the weapon with a smile that showed no envy, only joy for her good fortune. Her teacher crossed to the wall that held the school's weapons display and selected his own escrima sticks, then nodded to her. "If you intend to take an active role in the doings of this city, you must train harder, Caliste."

She split her weapon, the process happening automatically at her will, and barked a short laugh. "Yes, that seems to be the general consensus, Sensei."

"Excellent. Practice blocking." He shuffled in and brought his weapons around for slow strikes from every angle. Soon, the speed tripled and she sweated to keep up. He paused, and she recovered her balance. "Good basics but room for improvement. Now, hit me."

There was no chance of her meeting that demand, but that wasn't the point of the exercise. She attacked conservatively and guarded against a counter. At first, he simply deflected the blows. Then, he changed strategies and used blocks angled to impede her following attack. He launched an occasional riposte that required her to dodge out of the way but mainly, he seemed to be testing her. Finally, he stepped back and lowered his sticks to his sides to signal a stop. She panted as sweat dripped from her face.

"From now on, you come thirty minutes earlier to prepare the space. Then, we spend an hour with the sticks before class begins. Your skills are good, but you have the potential to be far better. When you show progress with them, we'll add the staff and the sword."

She bowed with deep respect. "Thank you, Sensei."

He grinned as her gaze lifted. "Wipe your sweat from the mat and prepare for class. You'll need to eat more and drink more from now on in order to maintain your energy."

Cali sighed and decided she needed to make sure Ikehara and Emalia never met one another, or her to-do list would stretch to infinity.

Given the success of their time at the dojo, she decided she could probably bring the Draksa to the tavern without any undue ruckus. She checked first for the usual issues—could he handle being indoors that long, could he deal with the noise and people, and could he avoid eating the dwarf behind the bar except on command? He grinned throughout, sat primly on her bed, and replied, "I would like nothing more. Your room is boring. Perhaps we can discuss a better one with your owner."

She frowned. "I don't have an owner."

He tilted his head to the side. "You don't do work for this dwarf?"

"Yes, I do."

"So, owner."

Exasperated, she put her hands on her hips. "He pays me and I use the money for things like food for you and to rent a roof over our heads."

Fyre raised a paw and examined the claws at the end of it. "So, you have someone who provides you with food and shelter but not an owner?"

She scowled. "Indirectly provides that stuff."

"An indirect owner."

"Okay, shut it, you." Mist came out of his nose as he snorted at her, and something obvious smacked her in the brain. "Holy hell. You and I need to train together."

The look he gave her was mixed interest and condescension in equal parts. "Well, of course. I wondered when you'd get around to that."

"I've been busy, and I'm sorry I haven't found out more about your kind yet. But clearly, you're equipped for fighting. Is that something you enjoy?"

His grin was pure evil. "Definitely."

"How does it normally work?"

He twitched his tail. "I presume you mean in partnership with someone like you?"

"No, as the sidekick to Aquaman. Of course that's what I mean."

His body rippled in what she'd come to recognize was his version of a shrug. "It depends on the partners. We are usually the close-up fighters, while the more breakable one attacks from range. You seem to prefer to charge in without concern for safety, so we might choose to fight side by side."

She laughed. "Yeah. You got me there. Let's do this the easy way." She summoned a portal that connected the room to the basement of the tavern and led him through. As it closed behind them, she noticed that the crates were stacked differently than they had been and muttered, "Bartender magic." She pointed at the Draksa. "You stay here. I want Zeb to give the okay before you pretend to be a dog upstairs."

He hopped up onto two crates that lay beside each other and sat with an aloof expression. She shook her head and mounted the stairs. As she was early, Janice was still there, wiping the mostly empty tables in preparation for the night crowd. Her gritted teeth hurt as she waved at the other woman and crossed to the bar. "Uh, could you come downstairs for a second? There's someone I'd like you to meet."

Zeb gave her a confused look, shrugged, and slipped out under one of the pass-throughs. She led him down without a word, stepped beside the Draksa, and waited for his response.

In all her time at the Drunken Dragons Tavern, she had never seen awe on her boss' face. Serenity, amusement, condescension a couple of times, and fury only once, but never something approaching reverence. It transformed him and made him look young as he approached the creature slowly. He raised a hand cautiously, and the dragon lowered his snout to sniff and push against it. *Again, like a cat. How is that even possible?*

The dwarf ran his fingers along his flank, his eyes still wide and feasting on the vision in front of him. She sighed. "You'll give him delusions of grandeur. Cut it out. Zeb, this is Fyre. Fyre, Zeb. We hoped he could stay upstairs while I work tonight. He's good at staying out of the way and can disguise himself really well. He could hang out at the top of the stairs and not cause any trouble."

The proprietor stepped back and let his hand drop with clear reluctance. "Show me," he demanded roughly. The Draksa shimmered and in a moment, was replaced by a handsome brown and white boxer with a collar and tag. He managed to find his usual gruff tone and said. "Yes. He can stay behind the bar with me. Let's go, beastie."

Fyre was up the stairs in a flash with Zeb marching after him. She was fairly sure she hadn't imagined the haughty expression on the dog's face as he went past, and she shook her head. *Great, upstaged by a dog. Dragon. Lizard. Thing. The only way tonight could be any better is if he decided to have Janice stay and help bartend.*

CHAPTER TWENTY-SIX

Cali drummed her fingers on the table while she waited for Tanyith to arrive. She'd chosen a random bar for the meeting, simply another tourist trap in the quarter, as she felt the need to keep tonight's business away from the Dragons. A cranberry and tonic, her drink of choice for nights out when she wasn't surrounded by people she trusted, sat before her untouched. Her shift had gone well, and Zeb had seemed more his usual self, but she had the looming sense that walls were closing in to constrain her choices and didn't like it.

In fact, she disliked it so much that she'd felt the need to meet with Tanyith in person. A series of texts had arranged the time and place and now, she waited, having arrived early. Her phone buzzed with a text from Dasante, who played lookout between sessions of three-card monte with a couple of his friends as assistants on the street outside. Her gaze was on the opening that replaced the bar's front wall when the man walked through it.

He looked freshly showered with his hair pulled back

into a ponytail. Black jeans and boots were worn with a white button-down, the long sleeves rolled below the elbows. His beard and mustache showed signs of having finally been attended to by a professional. All in all, if she was ten years older and had a crush on Thor, he might have landed in her pool of potential dates. She laughed to herself. *Damn shallow pool, Cal.*

Her partner stopped at the bar for a glass of his own, something involving clear liquid from a bottle and a stream from the soda gun. Lime slices suggested a gin and tonic, which was a drink she could respect. She didn't think highly of people who ordered fruity drinks based on long experience at the Dragons. Pina Coladas were also out, given their popularity on Bourbon Street. He slid into the seat across from her. "Hey."

She rolled her eyes with a small smile and tried to force some positivity into her words. "Thanks for coming."

The way his face went blank signaled his protective walls snapping into position, and he leaned in closer. "What's going on?"

Cali shook her head. "I got into a ruckus the other day with some of the Zatoras. They planned to burn down my Aikido school, and I happened to be in the right place at the right time. I disguised myself, but both Detective Barton and my teacher figured out it was me."

"How?"

"Traffic cameras for her, the way I fight for him. It turns out he had a security camera on the alley."

"Is everything okay with your Sensei?"

She nodded. "Better than. I have to show up early to get

the place ready, but he'll spend time training me to use the sticks before class."

"Why sticks?"

She realized he hadn't been let in on that secret yet and raised her wrists to display the bracelets. "Magic weapons from Zeb."

He whistled softly. "You have solid people in your corner, Cali. I've never even seen a magical weapon, much less used one."

"That's not true. I'm positive that Valerie is magical, too."

"What's up with that guy?" He frowned a little. "A Dwarf with a magic ax? Shouldn't he be out there mixing it up with the bad guys instead of you?"

Cali chuckled. "You'll have to discuss that with him. All I'll say is that he claims to have a philosophical objection to violence."

"And owns a battleax."

"Yes."

"So, is that all you wanted to talk about?" He'd dropped the flirting attempts, mostly, which she welcomed.

"No. We need to get our plans together. The deadline is only two days away for the heist."

He laughed. "You've been watching too many detective movies. Next up, you'll be saying 'gumshoe' and 'caper.'"

Her phone buzzed with three texts in a row, and she sighed as she read the warning. "How about copper?" She tilted her head toward the window and he turned in time to watch Kendra Barton come through the entrance.

The representative of the NOPD was in street clothes—jeans, and a t-shirt plus her standard boots. She declined to visit the bar and instead, came to their table, snagged an unused chair from a different one, spun it, and sat reversed on it. She folded her arms on the top. "So, Caliste, who's your friend?"

"So, Detective Barton, how did you find me here? I'm fairly sure there are no traffic cameras here in the quarter."

She grinned unashamedly. "Foot surveillance. You really need to pay more attention to what's going on around you." She extended a hand to Tanyith. "Since she doesn't seem interested in introducing us, I'm Kendra."

He shook it and nodded. "John. John Doe."

The detective laughed. "Okay, John. Pleased to meet you." She leaned back to regard them both. "So, what are you up to tonight? Also, not to be rude, but he's a little old for you."

Cali rolled her eyes and Tanyith shook his head. She said, "We're merely friends having a drink."

"You could have done that at the Dragons."

"You don't seem to spend much time at your workplace. What makes you think I want to be at mine during my rare free moments?"

She didn't answer but turned to Tanyith. "Where do you work, John?"

His lips twitched. "Here and there."

Barton frowned. "I feel like I should know you." She drummed her fingers on the table, then snapped them. "You were part of the Atlantean gang a couple of years ago, right?"

Cali burst into laughter and patted him on the shoulder. "She does that—tries to make it seem as if she didn't have the information ahead of time. The truth is she probably saw you with me at some point and looked you up."

The woman nodded. "Guilty as charged. So, back with your old crew?"

He scowled and his voice rasped. "No. I'm nothing like them."

She shrugged. "If you say so. I'm not sure the sight of you two together does much for my state of mind, though. You're an allegedly former gang member, and she's targeted by at least one gang, maybe more." Barton looked at her. "Are you safe? I can take you out of here and into protective custody. You only need to say the word."

"I'm great. Feel free to run along now."

"I don't think so. How about, instead, you tell me what you two are up to? In return, you won't have to spend the night in separate cells."

Cali knew it was an empty threat, but her instincts told her to trust the woman, at least a little. "Fine. We're trying to find a way to protect our places from the expanding gangs."

The detective nodded. "Ikehara's."

Tanyith added, "And the Dragons." At Cali's gesture, he continued, "We've watched some low-level people and seen where they go and who they talk to. It let us determine the headquarters for the Atlanteans—The Shark Nightclub."

"Interesting. We've had that on our radar for some time, but they've never stepped out of line enough to go in and take a look."

Cali barked a laugh. "You have someone follow me but you can't manage one of those trucks outside with a huddle of sweaty policemen listening in? You may not be using your resources well, lady."

Barton clapped sharply. "Is that all you have? Because it's not really weighting the scales all the way to the side that keeps you out of jail tonight."

He nodded. "Abuse of power never changes, I see."

She gave him a thin grin. "Only a little one. It's more like stretching the rules a teensy bit. Does that sound familiar to you two?"

Ouch. Yeah, maybe. Especially with what's coming in a couple of days. Cali sighed. "We've told you everything that's relevant to your area. You know about the Atlanteans. You know that the guys outside the dojo were Zotaras. You know we've been watching. What more do you want?"

"Tell me why you're here tonight. And don't say it's social."

"Okay. I asked him to meet me to tell him I'd been found out by you and my teacher for the alley thing, and to think of a way how to avoid being noticed in the future. It seems to be going really well, by the way."

Barton chuckled. "Your secret's safe with me. But this is the place where I tell you to back off and leave it to the professionals."

Cali growled with real annoyance. "You told me to do this. You wanted to 'use me,' remember?" She ignored Tanyith's head whipping around in reaction to her words.

"No." The detective's voice had lowered but was no less forceful. "I asked you to keep your ears open. I definitely didn't tell you to start fights with gang members. That's a little beyond minimal rule abuse and into active malfeasance."

Tanyith jumped into the conversational gap. “Okay, let’s back down a little. We all want the same thing. There’s no need to get spiky on one another.” He leaned forward. “If we hear anything useful, we’ll share it with you. Let’s keep the lines of communication open.” He gave her his cell number, and she recorded it on her phone.

Cali was a little less growly but not completely so. “‘Quid pro quo, Clarice,’ remember?” Her Hannibal Lecter impersonation was lacking but the meaning was there.

Barton nodded. “I remember. I don’t have much you don’t already know. The only information that borders on your area of interest is already obvious. Territories are in flux.”

“Do you have any people on the docks?” he asked,

She shrugged. “Some. Petty crooks on a leash, mainly, and not too trustworthy.”

“We wouldn’t need much. Only when a boat with Atlanteans was coming in. I imagine the innocent ones use the cruise ships. The criminals probably get portaled in.”

“What do you need with them?”

“Some questions and answers about New Atlantis.”

Her brow narrowed. “What does that have to do with anything?”

“I won’t know until I have the conversation.”

The detective tapped her fingers on the table, then stood abruptly. “Okay. I’ll get you what I can. But you’d better have something to trade for it.” She left without another word and threaded through the crowd with only the occasional shoulder-bump to clear the way.

Cali looked at Tanyith. “Nice redirection.”

He shrugged. “I’m often the peacemaker.”

"You don't seem like the type."

"So I've heard."

She raised an eyebrow. "You look distracted. Are you thinking about Kendra?"

"Who?" He sounded startled.

"Detective Barton. Kendra. Don't think I missed the heavy eye contact between you two. I can't wait to tell Dasante you have a crush on a cop." She rose and headed to the front, relishing the stunned expression on her partner's face. *Maybe it's time to add matchmaker to my resume.*

CHAPTER TWENTY-SEVEN

She had dodged to one side at the sight of the limousine on the street outside. It wasn't the right part of town for such a ride, much less the right nightspot. Cali caught Dasante's eye and gave him the signal to bail using a modified version of the buskers' secret language. He and his friends made some noise about the lame customers and ambled away.

Tanyith whispered in her ear from behind. "Trouble?"

"Who brings a limo here?"

"Bachelor party?"

"Nah, they'd be up on Bourbon. Do you think this place has a back way out?"

She kept her eyes forward and sighed as he confirmed her fears. "Yeah. But there's a guy in a suit standing in the doorway to the restrooms, which is where it probably is."

"Damn. That is not good."

"Can you illusion us out of here?"

Irritated, she turned to him. "I could, but if they were able to locate us here, they could doubtless trace us back, which would put others in danger. They might only be after me because of the alley." The conclusion that it was the human gang was the only thing that fit the visible pieces of the puzzle. "I'll head out and go right. You go left. If they only grab me, it's up to you to find me. I'm sure Barton will help."

He nodded. "And if they take both of us?"

"Dasante and I have a code. If he doesn't hear from me by morning, he'll create some noise about it. At least that's something."

"It's nice to have friends."

Cali slapped him on the shoulder. "You'll make a friend eventually. Maybe Kendra can introduce you to some of hers." She turned, took a deep breath, and made her move.

Her right turn led her into the chest of a tall, muscular man in a suit that seemed a size too small for him. She looked up. "Um, excuse me?"

He grumbled, "Into the car, miss. No trouble. We wouldn't want any bystanders to get hurt."

She sighed. *Yeah, unless you're heartless or Captain Marvel, that threat will usually work.* "Okay. You'll drop me here after?"

His only response was a thin smirk as he gestured back the way she'd come. She turned and saw Tanyith escorted into the limousine. *Damn.* She'd no sooner climbed into the rear beside him when the two who had intercepted them piled in and sat on the opposite side with their backs to the driver. The seats were white leather, with tinted windows all around, including behind the guards. There was a short delay she attributed to waiting for the one who'd been positioned to block their exit in the other direction before the car lurched into motion.

Tanyith buckled his seatbelt, leaned back, and closed his eyes. "So, that went great, I think."

She did the same. "Yep. Where do you think we're headed?"

"Well, these guys certainly aren't the brains of the outfit, so I assume we're on the way to wherever he or she is."

"I wonder if the cop who tracked me is on their payroll. If not, at least someone knows where we went. Hell, I guess a whole bar full of people knows where we went."

A growl came from the seat opposite. "Shut up you two. Another word and we start breaking fingers."

The fear crawling up her back threatened to emerge in laughter, and she threw it in the corner of her mind and wrapped a double portion of crime scene tape around it. She forced herself to think rather than react and had a dozen potential ideas for escape put together by the time the car finally stopped half an hour later. The door opened from the outside, and a mansion appeared in front of them. It was lit by spotlights on the ground and roof and surrounded by opulent greenery with its own illumination. It was an absolutely beautiful piece of real estate and an important part of New Orleans history that she recognized instantly.

Inside it was the thing they'd been ordered to steal. They were outside the home base of the Zatora crime syndicate.

The obligatory preliminaries had been taken care of quickly and effectively, depriving Tanyith of his pocketknife and both of them of their cell phones. Her bracelets remained on her wrists, which at least meant that piece of information hadn't gotten back to the boss. *Or they think they can handle it if I decide to use them, which is definitely the scarier proposition.*

Beyond the foyer was a massive room, easily eight times the size of hers at the boarding house. A large sweeping staircase dominated the view, with elegant chandeliers hanging down from the ceiling two stories above. To the right were two couches that looked more comfortable than her bed and to the left, a pool table and several dark wood tables to complement it. Men in suits wandered freely, some clearly working and others with drinks in their hands and smiles on their faces. *Well, it is one-thirty in the morning. It stands to reason that only the revelers are still up.*

She snuck a look at Tanyith and received a quick shake of his head in return. All she could do was trust he'd find a way to let her know if he was about to make a move, and she planned to not need his help if she chose to act. They were escorted along the short hallway that ran to the right of the staircase, past a powder room and to a set of stairs leading downward. Their guards were smart. One preceded them to watch them from the bottom, while the other kept his distance at the top.

In the basement, another short hallway led to a door. The faint sound of motors suggested equipment keeping the lower level free from the moisture that had to surround it. *I bet that's expensive.* The first man knocked softly, his ear to the wood panel. He twisted the handle and stepped through the opening. A comfortable living room lay within, and a man with a laptop sat on one of the two couches set at a right angle to one another. The guards guided them with surprisingly gentle touches to sit on the unused couch, as far from him as possible. One guard took a seat on the couch next to the man, his posture rigid and alert, and the other stood at the opposite corner of the arrangement.

The laptop snapped closed, and its owner set it aside. The man crossed his legs and the expensive fabric of his grey pinstripe custom suit aligned perfectly. He wore a white button-down with the top button undone. Intelligence and determination radiated from him. *Brad Pitt will look like this guy in a decade or two.* His speech was smooth and clear. "I'm Rion Grisham. Thank you both for coming."

Cali laughed. "You didn't leave us much of a choice."

"Indeed. I did not. Let that be an initial lesson to you. I always get what I want. It's merely a matter of the amount of pain required to achieve it."

Tanyith asked, "So, what is it that you want with us?"

Their host nodded. "I appreciate directness and will return it in kind. We have noticed you both at the Drunken Dragons Tavern. You more than him, naturally, Ms Leblanc."

She refused to give him the pleasure of seeing her react to the use of her name. "Yes, I work there. That's not a state secret or anything."

He tilted his head and his eyes burned into hers to communicate his view of her attitude. She swallowed hard but didn't flinch. "Of course not. It's easily discovered. But what is immediately relevant is your influence on the owner, one Zarden. You could convince him to agree to our proposal. We would be willing to reduce the payment to a nominal fee in order to have the establishment clearly on our side of the line."

To control the instinctive rebuttal, she cleared her throat. "Have you…uh, discussed this with him?"

The man sighed. "The representative I sent mentioned something about an ax—a large ax, I believe."

Cali shook her head. "If Zeb isn't into it, it probably won't happen."

"I imagine you could convince him if you were properly motivated. Surely I don't need to explain the reasons you should be interested in helping us." The threat to her, to Tanyith, and likely to her friends and family had been understood from the moment she'd seen the limo.

"No, I get it. What if I can't convince him to agree?"

"Then I'll have to take a more difficult path and you shall reap the rewards of your failure. Or, I should say, others will."

The surge of magic that flowed to her hands at the second bald threat to her loved ones required a moment of focus to control. While she pushed it back, she realized that hers was not the only magic in the room. If felt like an echo, something barely sensed. She tried to catch hold of it but failed. Her frown from the threat covered her reaction to the revelation, fortunately. "Understood. I'll do what I can."

He nodded. "Do more." His attention shifted to Tanyith. "And you. If you fail to accomplish this with her, you'll be back in Trevilsom. This time, underground. Don't doubt that I know people who can make that happen."

Her partner stiffened and she put a hand on his arm. He shrugged it off reflexively but maintained his position. The trembling in his fingers was the only outward sign of his internal struggle. He managed to respond roughly. "Gotcha."

The man smiled, the kind of aggravating grin that only those who knew others were powerless to hurt them were capable of. It hovered in her vision during the walk back to the car and the drive to the quarter and infuriated her more with each passing minute.

When they were released from the limo, she lifted a finger to her lips, held her phone out, and pointed at him. He handed his over, and she put them both next to the jukebox that belted out Jimmy Buffett before she pulled him to the other side of the room. With her mouth beside his ear, she whispered, "They could have bugged them while they had them. Your knife too."

He nodded.

"Did you notice the magical?" He gave her a quizzical look and shook his head. "There was something or someone in the room. I sensed it when my magic tried to escape to separate that bastard's skull from the rest of him." Her body took that statement as a cue to drop the adrenaline that had sustained her, and she sat quickly before she fell.

"Are you okay?"

She waved his concern away and motioned him down so she could whisper. "I will be. But Zeb would only agree to this for me and I can't let him do that. We need to find a way to beat them at their own game."

His frown was immediate, and he put his mouth at her

ear. "So, it's not enough to double-cross one of the two biggest gangs in New Orleans, your plan is to do it to both?"

It sounded better in my head. She shrugged. "Yeah, basically."

"This should be stupendous." He laughed. "We might as well get some sleep and start early, right?"

Her grin was almost mechanical. "Seriously, dude, find someone your own age to hit on."

He waved as he retrieved his phone and headed to the exit. *Maybe someday, we'll both have time to find someone to date. But that sure as hell isn't this day.*

CHAPTER TWENTY-EIGHT

Cali had lucked out in the timing of her late night, as she wasn't scheduled at the dojo the next day. Sleeping in had been blissful, and she'd stayed that way into the early afternoon. Fyre had tried to rouse her, but she was wise to his tricks and put a force barrier around herself without coming more than half awake. There was no doubt in her mind that he could have banished it if he'd wanted to but fortunately, he must have understood her need for some solid rest.

The Draksa hung out behind the bar again during the evening shift at the tavern and was still there when Tanyith appeared moments before closing for their strategy session. She had decided not to explain all the details but rather to simply inform Zeb they needed a solution immediately to ensure the tavern's safety. When she'd told him, he'd nodded and agreed to talk about it later.

And now, later had arrived. She locked the door and he drew three ciders and placed them on the bar. He said briskly, "Fyre," and the Draksa, in his normal form, raised his snout in time to catch the stream of soda water Zeb shot at him. The dwarf had quickly discovered his bar's mascot loved the stuff and that it caused him to belch frost breath, which for no apparent reason was hilarious to her boss. Truth be told, she was barely able to keep a straight face. The sight of the two of them playing together filled her soul with sunshine.

She sipped and approved of his choice of soft versions of the drink for them all. They had a little over two days left to fulfill the demands of the Atlanteans, and although a timetable hadn't been placed on the other demand, every plan she'd come up with put that action in the same timeframe.

A short silence had settled in so she cleared her throat. "Okay, the only way I can see this working is if we somehow pit them against one another. Make it so they have to back off or lose face. Barton said that the leaders are both fairly new, so they won't be able to afford to look bad."

The men both nodded, seemingly content to let her lay out the situation. "The Atlanteans told us to steal a pair of pistols from the Zatoras. Clearly, that's a shot at the human gang with complete deniability on their part." More nods greeted this statement. "And the humans want the tavern on their side. The problem is if we do that, this place becomes a battleground. We have to find a solution that gives them both a win or an equal loss but doesn't sacrifice our ability to stay the hell out of their mess."

Zeb nodded. "I have friends around who speak for certain magical groups. They are agreed that we need to try to control the spread of their influence where we can but not so much that we risk all-out war between them. It would suck everyone in, which would not be good for anyone."

Cali stared at the Dwarf. *That sounds like it was an interesting conversation. I wonder what else I don't know about him.* He met her gaze with a small smile that suggested he knew what she was thinking and enjoyed being mysterious. She sighed. "I have an idea, but I'm not sure it's a good idea."

Tanyith chuckled. "Bad might be the best we can get, at this point. Spill."

"If we steal the pistols, we make Rion Grisham look bad. If we sign on with them, we tick the Atlanteans off. What we need to do is make them both look equally bad and be the middle people to help them save face in exchange for leaving us alone."

Zeb shrugged and lit his pipe before he spoke. Between puffs, he asked, "What can you do to mess up the Atlanteans' image?"

She turned to the ex-member of that gang. "What would do it?"

He thought about it for a second, then smiled. "It would all have to be even. Since we'll go into the Zatora headquarters, I guess we'll need to make a return appearance at The Shark Nightclub."

"There's something there that would work?"

His shrug was offhand. "I couldn't tell you for sure, but it stands to reason there'd be valuables in that nice office, doesn't it?"

A slow grin grew on her face. "I think I'll enjoy this." His expression matched hers as he nodded, and they both turned to the dwarf. Cali said, "So, Zeb, do you see any problems?"

He blew several smoke rings. "Obviously, you'll need to go in disguised, even though it won't hold up for long. Maybe you'll get lucky and the boss won't be there. I wonder if there's a way to turn that to our advantage too."

"Anything that causes confusion to our enemies is a good thing," Tanyith agreed. "But if the goal is to find someone specific to impersonate, we're definitely running out of time."

"Maybe that's where we loop Barton in. I bet she has intelligence on both groups," she added quickly.

Zeb nodded. "So, if you masquerade as the opposite side and make sure you're seen, they'll automatically have somewhere to place the blame. That's good. But it puts those people in danger, which isn't so good."

Cali took another sip and held her glass out for a refill. "I thought the same thing." Her boss took the glass and twisted to the cask as she continued. "What if Barton picked them up while it was all going down or even beforehand if she could? She could put them in protection or something. They might be inclined to give evidence in that case, too. At worst, they'll at least have to leave town."

Tanyith looked uncomfortable when he spoke. "That's fairly harsh for them."

The dwarf set the glass down in front of Cali a little louder than required and took the man's to top it off. "Then you'll need to make sure the ones who get that treatment deserve it."

She nodded. "Again, I think the detective can help us there. So, any other issues?"

Neither of her companions spoke, and she smiled. "Okay. First thing tomorrow, I'll connect with her, and Tanyith can take a look at the places and pull together any gear needed for the jobs. They're expecting us to move on Friday, so we'll do it on Thursday instead and defuse the situation the next day. Does that sound good?"

They nodded simultaneously, and she smiled, remembering the days of watching old television shows with her father. "I love it when a plan comes together."

CHAPTER TWENTY-NINE

Kendra Barton had been less happy to see her than Cali had expected. When she'd sauntered through the police station and into the office, the other woman had been ensconced behind her desk, typing angrily on the black keyboard that failed to coordinate with the beige monitor above it. At the sight of her, the detective thumped a final key with more force than necessary and leaned back in her chair.

"It's too early for your nonsense, Caliste. What do you want?"

She raised an eyebrow as she slid into the seat next to the desk, fully aware that making it obvious she was staying would irritate her even more. "I thought we could have a chat. A little this-for-that, right?" She leaned forward and stage-whispered, "I don't know the words you use. Am I an informant? Are you going to put me in the hoosegow?"

"You're an annoying brat, and I'll put you in the street

on your ass if you keep it up." The slight twitch of her lips suggested she wasn't completely serious.

Cali grinned and hoped it looked suitably provocative. "Okay, first, if you haven't had enough coffee, you should definitely find more. If you have had a few, you should think about cutting back. This is not how you make friends. Maybe you and Tanyith could join some kind of support group to learn how to interact with other humans."

Barton folded her arms, stared, and growled her irritation. "Get to the point."

"I need something from you and in return, I have something for you. An opportunity. But you'll want to ask questions, and I won't be able to answer them as fully as you'd like. Are you okay with that?"

"Keep talking."

"First, I need to know if you have surveillance on the gangs in town. I'm sure you do, but I need to confirm it."

The woman nodded.

"So you're the strong, silent type. Okay, now I get the picture. Speaking of pictures, I need some. I'm looking for two people in the human gang who are basically on the lower end of things but who you'd like to get off the streets. The same for the Atlanteans."

The detective let her arms drop to the desktop as she leaned forward. "Why do you need them?"

Cali shook her head. "That's one of the subjects I can't answer fully."

"And by fully you mean at all? That won't fly, Caliste."

She forced herself to relax and to trust. "Okay, look. I'm in a little deeper than I'd like to be and I have to do something about it. In order to do that, I need a disguise. It makes sense to use someone who's already a scumbag since this will mess up their lives. In fact, you'll probably want to pick them up while the..." She paused as her protective instincts caught up. "While stuff is going down. For their protection."

Barton frowned. "So you're planning to impersonate these people and do something that will tick the gangs off."

"It doesn't sound as good when you say it. But yeah, that's the plan."

The woman lowered her forehead to the desk and a tapping noise accompanied the bone meeting the wood. Her expression was hidden by the angle and the dark hair that fell across the point of impact. After four times, she raised it and met her visitor's eyes. "You'll get yourself hurt. Or killed. And worse, you'll get me fired for going along with it."

Cali shrugged. "We have to do what we have to do, with or without your help. It's safer with it, but I'll understand if you don't think you can. Tell me now rather than waste time I can use to adapt."

Barton frowned. "You said 'we.' Who's we? You and the blonde guy with the beard?"

"You know his name. Why do you do that?"

The detective laughed. "I learned it from watching *Columbo*. Answer the question."

"Yes, Tanyith."

"Okay. Let's say I agree to help with this insanity. What's in it for me?"

She'd discussed this detail with the other two briefly the night before prior to their leaving and going their separate ways. They'd added to her initial idea and agreed it should be persuasive. *I guess we'll find out.* "You get gang members off the street who ideally might give you information but who will definitely want to leave town afterward. So, immediate cleanup. People care about statistics, right? That's a cop thing? Mark down four for you."

Barton shook her head. "I could do that without you. We generally let the small ones run until they can bring us bigger fish, and this is a fairly tiny catch."

Cali sighed. "Okay, also, what we'll do will set both gangs back, at least for a while. It'll be safer out there for everyone."

"So you say. Do you care to offer proof? Evidence? Details of what you're planning, maybe?"

"No, that's not an option."

"You're not planning to kill anyone, are you?" The detective frowned.

"Holy mother of Megazon, what the hell, woman?" The yelped words were out before her brain knew they were coming. She lowered her voice. "No. Definitely not."

Barton's lips twitched. "I'd say that's a wholly honest answer. It could be the first you've given me. Ever." She frowned. "What else?"

Cali exhaled an exasperated breath. "I'm not sure if you're already aware of this because I wasn't until last night. Apparently, there's a group of magical beings that gathers as kind of a team, or committee, or something. They want to see action taken. I'm told your support will be noticed and appreciated, which could mean better information flow in the future."

"That's all fairly vague."

"Four losers off the streets is reason enough, and you know it. Anything else is merely a bonus."

The detective stared, probably hoping for more from her, but she was fresh out of items to offer. Her backup plan was not nearly as good. She was perilously close to convincing herself to plead for the woman's assistance when she finally spoke.

"Okay. I'll help you. But I'll need the details on when and where things are going down so I can have people ready to roll in case it all goes to hell."

"Yeah, promise first. And no takebacks."

Barton rolled her eyes. "You have my word."

She extended a hand. "Shake on it." The other woman's palm slid into hers, and she tasted the familiar pineapple-banana flavor that told her the detective was suspicious but being honest. The hint of anise at the edges suggested she wouldn't respond well to being deceived, however.

When she released the woman's hand, she smiled. "The Shark Nightclub and the Zatora mansion. Tonight."

The officer leaned back with a sigh. "No offense, but you're crazy, and I kind of wish I'd never met you."

Cali laughed. "No takebacks."

"Just so I'm completely clear, there's no way I can talk you out of this?"

She shook her head and turned serious. "No. It's necessary to protect the people I care about. We've gone through the options and this is the only one with a decent chance to accomplish that."

"I could lock you up for your own protection."

"Sure. But then Tanyith and Zeb would have to do it without me, and they aren't as good at disguise. And before you say it, if I don't text them a code by a certain time, they'll both fade so you can't find them."

Barton ran her hands through her hair. "You've certainly thought this through. Fine. So be it. When do you need the pictures?"

"Now would be helpful."

"Whoever made you this annoying should be slapped." She sighed and pressed keys on her keyboard. "All right, let's get ourselves some scumbags."

CHAPTER THIRTY

Emalia shook her head. "No, you need to concentrate more."

Cali rubbed her arm where the older woman had smacked her with a cane she occasionally used for show. Fyre was asleep on the floor, and the illusion she'd placed to make him look like the man Tanyith would be impersonating wavered into solidity in the afternoon sunlight coming through the window. *Damn it. If I can't hold the image in my guardian's living room against the dire threat of her walking stick, how will I do it and fight at the same time?* "I hear you. It was only a slip. It won't happen again."

The other woman folded her arms and nodded primly. "We'll see. Maybe you should consider a backup plan." It wasn't intended as an insult, surely, but it registered as one.

She gritted her teeth and locked the illusions that masked her and the Draksa safely away in compartments of her mind, doubled the barriers that held them in place, and pictured a constant flow of magic trickling to them. "Okay. Let's do it."

Her mentor raised her hand and targets appeared in the air around her, small spinning vortexes of energy.

The student pointed her finger and dispatched a bolt of force at each. They were consumed on impact and the target spun into nothingness. She eliminated all of them, only to face another group, larger and more plentiful than the first. With two fingers, she fired more powerful bolts. Her teacher often criticized her need for physical gauges of power and called it a bad habit. *One more thing to add to the to-do list, right?*

While she was distracted, the cane rapped her on the cheek. She growled and held her focus to remove targets one after the other as Emalia smacked the wooden rod into her legs, arms, and ultimately, over the top of her head. Finally, both the attacks and targets vanished, and she glanced at the Draksa. The illusion of a man sleeping on the floor, while certainly strange, was intact and believable. It brought a smile to her face.

She looked back to find Emalia wearing the same grin. "Good work, child. You're ready. There's only one thing left to do."

The front door was latched, the *closed* sign in place, and Cali sat across the small table from her teacher. Fyre was curled under the ebony tablecloth that reached almost all the way to the floor. The crystal ball was put away, replaced by an ornate box Emalia had retrieved from a locked and warded chest in the corner. It was black-lacquered and had watercolor flowers painted on the top and sides. She lifted the lid and withdrew a black silk parcel. Setting the box to the side, she unfolded the protective fabric to reveal her tarot cards. They were unlike any set Cali had ever seen, aquatic-themed and dark except for neon flourishes visible in the black light from above. Her mind wandered as Emalia spread them out and shuffled them in a ritual only she understood.

Dasante had asked once if she always knew what was going to happen because her guardian was a real fortune-teller. She'd laughed and said the woman refused to read her, and the discussion had faded under other topics. The truth was more complicated. Her mentor had explained that there was danger inherent for both parties involved in repeated full readings, and so they'd agreed to limit their sessions. Her last had been before accepting the job at the Dragons and had resulted in one of the best decisions of her life.

Without a doubt, tonight rose to that level of importance. Emalia closed her eyes and intoned, "Focus your mind on your question." She pictured the plans for the night's activities and imagined the actions like examining a crystal for flaws, turning it this way and that to expose each facet to the light.

The fortune-teller's voice took over, deeper and more resonant than her guardian's normal speaking tone. "We beseech the universe for knowledge from the Clouds," She placed a card face-down. "Knowledge from the Land." Another card found its place, and Cali recognized the Compass pattern. "Knowledge from the Heavens." North, East, and South were now in position. "Knowledge from the Depths." As she spoke the final words, she set the last card face-down in the center. "Knowledge from the waters, the essence of life itself." Her eyes fluttered open and met her student's. "Let us see what the future has in store for you."

She flipped the rectangle furthest from her. It showed a man seated on a throne, a trident grasped in his hand. The weapon pointed away from Cali. "Your situation is represented by the emperor, inverted. From what you've told me, this is almost certainly the leader of the humans challenging you."

"That makes sense."

The next card, down and to the right, revealed a woman on a divan in a gown resembling waves and coral and who held an orb-topped scepter in her hand. Again, the object pointed away. "Empress, inverted, is your challenge." Emalia gazed at the image for a half-minute before she raised her eyes. "It could be the leader of the other faction. Or it could be something inside yourself that needs to be overcome."

The Draksa snorted, and Cali kicked him. "I'm sure it's the former. I'm clearly perfect."

There was a hint of a smile on her guardian's lips as she leaned forward again to the cards. "Guidance is next." She flipped the card on the west point of the Compass to discover Justice upright and chuckled. "Well, that one's clear."

A wave of confidence rolled through her, and she nodded in grateful agreement.

The next card, in the last cardinal direction, showed a man in robes wielding a wand to draw an infinity symbol in the air. Behind him appeared to be a city with a glimmering that might have been a dome above, through which dark sapphire ripples were visible. "The Magician, again inverted. You have the skills you need but may have to become more proficient in using them to succeed." Cali had nothing to say to that, so her mentor flipped the one in the center.

The High Priestess stared upward, draped in blue and wearing a hat consisting of a large pearl with fins to either side. It was upright, always a good sign. Emalia turned the positive into something less welcome with the reminder that while the High Priestess always signified growth, "Sometimes, the most effective growth comes from failure."

She sighed. "Thanks for ending on such an up note. Seriously, any more optimism and I might not be able to control myself."

The older woman smiled at her. "Perhaps it is not a night for control but for trusting instinct to see you through."

"Did you read that?" She frowned.

Emalia laughed. "No, I simply know you well, child. Please be reasonably careful." She lifted the cloth and looked under the table. "You keep her safe for me."

Fyre was still pretending not to speak when others were around, so he merely offered a nod with his snout. Cali rolled her eyes at him, gave her guardian a hug, and created a portal to take them to the tavern.

She and Fyre had availed themselves of the day's stew—

turkey, she thought, with tons of root vegetables and a spice she didn't recognize—and managed to nap on some crates in the basement while afternoon turned into evening. She, Zeb, and Tanyith agreed that midnight was the best time to start at the first location, and they should strike the other immediately after.

Which had been an open question prior to her reading. Now, she had decided to take them in order. She gave the sleeping Draksa a pat and yawned as she climbed the stairs. Janice was her usual annoying self in the common room, and Zeb maintained his usual serene presence behind the bar. The tavern was extra full tonight, more like a Friday crowd than a Thursday one, and an air of anticipation permeated the building. *Or maybe that's only me. Whatever.* The Dwarf slid a soft cider to her, and she drained it in a long draught and felt instantly better.

He looked at the door and she followed his gaze, so when Tanyith opened it and stepped inside, she saw his entrance. He'd slicked his hair into a ponytail, and his beard was tightly confined by a series of elastics. It was an entirely different and far more martial look for the man. The theme extended to his thick boots, tactical-style pants with big side pockets, and the tight black athletic shirt he wore. He carried a heavy-looking canvas sack over his shoulder. Zeb nodded and said, "You two can head to the basement. I'll be down shortly."

Cali followed him and at the bottom, he shrugged the bag onto a crate. A metallic clank sounded from it. She grinned. "Is that a sword in your pack or are you simply happy to see me?"

"Not quite." He laughed and shook his head as he loosened the drawstring and reached inside to withdraw two ornate hilts. He handed one of the sheaths to her, and she pulled the *sai* from it. The martial arts weapon looked like a spread trident in miniature—a steel blade with a sharp point in the middle and a curved prong to each side. She'd only seen practice versions before, and the wicked tips on all the ends proved that these were something else entirely. The blue leather of the grip was worn but otherwise, the weapon seemed well cared for.

"Nice. Did someone keep an eye on it for you while you were gone?"

"Kinda. They were buried in one of my treasure caches. My life wasn't really stable enough to settle down anywhere." He exhumed a brown leather belt from the bag and secured it around his waist, then attached the sheaths for the sai.

"No guns? I assumed you'd have guns too."

He shrugged. "It's not smart to get caught by the police with firearms. We always stuck to magic as our main weapon and hand to hand either for defense or to make a point."

"Which is it tonight?"

"Both." He smiled and retrieved a medium-sized wooden box from the bag. He set it on the crate and lifted the lid. Inside were two vials, one red and one blue. Above them, set at a right angle, was a folded piece of black fabric. He withdrew that first and showed how it unzipped to reveal a strip of gold coins, then pulled his shirt untucked to strap it around his stomach. "Backup plan one, in case we have to run."

Once he returned his outfit to its proper tucked

arrangement, he held up the red flask. "Health potion. Exhausting, but a literal lifesaver." He slid it into a loop on the side of his belt, then did the same with the other. "And an energy potion for when magic is running low."

She frowned. "Aren't they a little fragile to carry openly like that?"

"Nah. It's the same material bulletproof glass is made of."

Zeb's voice was unexpected. "You fancy young people. The old ways worked fine." He stepped off the bottom stair and headed to a corner of the room. She could barely make out his muttered, "Which crate is it in? Ah, right." He gestured and two of the boxes floated into the air so the bottommost could slide out from under them. Another motion removed the top from it. He pulled out a belt similar to Tanyith's in style but of black leather and far more broken-in. The dwarf handed it to her. "Your sticks should fit in the sheaths where my throwing axes went. They tie down to the legs."

She secured it and fastened the leg straps. "Nice. It feels good. Thank you."

He nodded and pulled a metal vial from each pocket. "I had a friend get these for you. They are specifically brewed for Atlanteans and should pack quite a kick." One had a cross engraved on the flip top and the other a star. She put the healing potion on her right hip in the loop that appeared custom made for that purpose, and the energy draught on her left.

"Thanks, Zeb. You know, for this and all the other stuff."

The dwarf waved dismissively. "Yeah, well, I can't send

my best worker out unprepared. I'd let you take Valerie, but she doesn't like anyone other than me." The idea of her carrying a battleax, much less swinging it, made her laugh. She presumed that was the cause of Tanyith's snort and scowled at him, which only caused his grin to grow wider.

Zeb gazed at them both without speaking for several seconds, then nodded. "You'll do. Be careful, and remember, if it gets hairy, come back here. I'll wait with the wards up but make sure no enemies follow you. I don't want to have to get Valerie dirty."

Cali resisted the urge to give him a hug. She'd save it for later when it was over. He stomped up the stairs, and she turned to her partner. "All right, Tay, are we ready for this?"

He nodded. "You know it."

She looked at her watch. They had twenty minutes until midnight. She grinned at him. "I hate waiting." She swung her attention to the Draksa, who had sat quietly in the corner as they finished gearing up. "You be prepared to eat anyone who follows us through."

He rose and extended his front paws as far forward as they could go with his rear end in the air. When he was done, he stretched his back legs one at a time. "I will if any get into our portals when we're leaving."

In her peripheral vision, Tanyith's head whipped around in surprise at the dragon's words. Cali frowned. "Come again?"

He sat in the center of the room. "I'm going with you, of course."

The man looked at her with an expression that clearly communicated, "This is your problem."

She shook her head. "I can't disguise you too. Maybe after I practice more or something…." Her words trailed off as Fyre vanished slowly from the ground up, the last thing to disappear his Cheshire cat grin. Cali put a hand over her face. "So. You can veil."

He reappeared wearing that "laughing at not laughing with" smile. Despite her love for the creature, she wanted nothing more than to slap him silly at that moment. She sighed. "You suck, you know that?"

"The two of you against entire gangs, pretending to be skilled thieves? You won't need me. Anyone can see that."

He wasn't wrong. "Fine. Be careful. I don't have a healing potion for you."

When she looked up, Tanyith was checking the draw on his weapons. She summoned her own and held them for a few extra seconds so they'd be ready to transform again before she slid them into their holders. The sticks fit perfectly. She concentrated on the pictures she'd spent the day memorizing and let her power reach toward her partner. His tanned skin darkened, his hair changed to black, and his beard became a goatee. The standard uniform of the Atlantean gang followed as his clothes transformed into jeans and a hoodie. "Move around," she commanded, and he jumped and waved his arms a few times. The illusion held, and she pushed it into a corner of her mind and willed magic to continue to flow to it.

Cali repeated the process on herself and became a tall, pale man with a ratty t-shirt, jeans, and sneakers. Long dreadlocks hung over the image's chest and back. "Check me." She moved around, and he nodded before she locked that spell down in her brain as well.

After a deep breath, she looked first at the Draska and then at Tanyith. "Let's get this nonsense over with, shall we?"

He opened a portal to a dark patch of grass, and they all stepped through together.

CHAPTER THIRTY-ONE

The mansion that served as the home base of the Zatora syndicate was uncomfortably bright, exactly as it had been during their involuntary reconnaissance a few nights before. The portal had deposited them about a hundred and fifty yards away from the front door, which was on a diagonal from their position. She manipulated the surrounding air to muffle their sounds and cast a veil in a small semicircle to keep them unseen.

A movement from below revealed that Fyre wore the body of a rottweiler. "Will you vanish or something?"

He offered her a doggy smile. "I'm letting you two see my disguise. No one else can. It's only in case there are problems with the veil."

She nodded and looked at Tanyith. "So, last chance to take Barton's offer and choose the safety of a jail cell."

He shook his head, and his game face gave her no indication whether he'd appreciated the joke. "Been there, done that. It's completely overrated. Let's mess up some gangsters instead."

"Okay. Your lead." It hadn't taken long to determine that he had skills and knowledge about breaking and entering she lacked.

"When I set up the portal earlier, I managed to look all the way around the house. There's a back door we can use." He walked in that direction and crouched behind cover where it was present despite the illusion masking them from sight. "Always over-prepare," he'd said during the planning sessions, and Zeb had agreed heartily.

"So, did you get a better sense of where the pistols are?"

His response sounded annoyed. "No, I didn't. There were no windows into the basement and too much traffic upstairs to see anything. But my guess is that he'd want them close, so we'll start with the office and maybe his bedroom."

"Okay. I don't suppose you have skills in mind reading or mind control or mind manipulation or something useful?"

He released a short laugh. It, too, sounded annoyed. "No. Is it possible for you to be quiet? We're on enemy territory here."

Fyre replied, "Not that I've seen. The greater the danger, the more words she has."

Cali growled a protest. "Shut it, both of you. There's a guard ahead."

In fact, there were two, roving outdoor patrols that had briefly come together mid-circuit from opposite directions. Tanyith said, "They'll do the same in the front. There are four guards. We'll have to sneak in quickly enough that they don't walk into us."

She closed her eyes for an instant and pulled the sight

and sound shields in tighter. They needed to get in unseen. At the right moment, they darted ahead, and she watched over Tanyith's shoulder as he stuck some kind of device into the lock. The Draksa pressed against her leg. A couple of seconds later, it clicked and he repeated the process with the deadbolt before they stepped hastily inside. He closed the door quietly behind them with no time to spare.

They'd anticipated seeing the same or fewer people milling about and so far, their luck was holding. Sounds of a billiards game came from the front, reduced mainly to impressions by the size of the home. Tanyith pointed to the left, and they advanced through a storage area before arriving at the junction with the hallway they'd traveled previously. He peeked around the corner and waved them forward, and they made it to the basement without incident.

He checked his blades again. "It's time."

She nodded and let the veil fall so their disguises would show. If the plan worked, they'd be seen on security cameras and the blame would fall on the other gang. At all costs, they had to have deniability, and maintaining the cover was her primary responsibility. As soon as someone saw them, the time for stealth would be over, so they had to move fast. Tanyith led the way to the office door at a run, pushed it open, and thrust into the room.

Rion Grisham was in there, again working at the couch. Two guards leaned against the walls and launched immediately in motion at the intrusion. She yelled, "Left," and headed to the one closest to the entry wall. Tanyith turned toward the one on the right, raised his hands, and discharged a shimmering blast of power that lifted the guard and thumped him into the wall. Her own target clawed for the pistol under his armpit when she punched the air and her force fist connected with his solar plexus. He dropped to a knee but maintained enough composure to get the gun out. She kicked it from his hand and put him in a chokehold that stole the rest of his breath. When she released him, he slumped to the ground unconscious.

Gunfire rang out as Grisham reacted slower than the others, but it was quickly silenced when the giant dog pounced on him. He cried out in fear, unable to see what was attacking him, which unexpectedly made her laugh. A burst of frost breath sealed the Zatora boss in a shimmering case of ice. She patted Fyre on the back. "Who's a good dog? You are, that's who."

He snorted with amusement, and she turned to help Tanyith search. Her partner ransacked the furniture in the room and opened every drawer and door. Locked ones received a blast of force magic that reduced them to splinters. She yanked paintings off the walls and moved the area rug that was under a table on the far side. Her partner emerged from the en suite bathroom shaking his head. "They aren't here."

She sighed. "So, we have to go upstairs."

"Yeah."

"And there are probably many more of them between here and there, by now."

"Also yeah."

Cali was struck by a sudden thought. "Hey, Fyre, you haven't mentioned being able to portal. I bet you can, though, right?"

"Of course."

"Okay. I have a plan. Tanyith, help me barricade the door."

They emerged from the rift in the same location where they'd arrived before. The house was awash in spotlights, but there was also clearly activity through the windows. The Draksa had been tasked with keeping up the appearance that they were trapped inside the office, and Cali had little doubt he would do an excellent job of it.

They ran under cover of a veil again, headed toward the side of the mansion, and stopped before the pool of light that covered the last dozen yards. Several upstairs windows were illuminated from within, but there was no visible activity in them. Getting to the house was the easy part, though. When they arrived, it was time for the hard part. She turned to Tanyith. "How good are you with force magic?"

"Extremely."

Damn. Why does he have to be so confident about it? "Then you'll have to do the throwing unless you can jump that high."

He stared at it. "No, I can't make that. Half that, tops."

"I couldn't even get that far. And I'd probably throw you into a wall."

"Okay, I see your point. How will you pull me up after you?"

She shrugged. "Maybe I'll find an escape rope or something. Otherwise, wait here and be prepared to save me if things go wrong. If you're in danger, bail and I can portal away. If I'm not out in ten minutes, same deal, and I'll meet you at the Tavern."

"Zeb won't let me leave the place alive if you get hurt. So don't. Are you ready?"

"Yeah." She took a deep breath. "As ready as I'm gonna be. Do it."

It was as if a giant hand took hold of her and hurled her upward. She was already casting as it started and summoned small shields of force on each palm which she held in front of her face and curled body as she impacted with the window. Glass shattered and the wooden braces splintered as she careened through. She bounded briefly on a bed but rolled off, landed on her side, and slid to a stop with a hard thump when she collided with the wall.

Her body wanted to pause and recover, but Cali forced herself into motion. She was in a feminine bedroom and discarded it as the likeliest hiding place. A door led to a hallway with several other doors in it. She whispered a plea to fate as she yanked the next one open, only to discover it was a knitting room of some kind with an actual spinning wheel in the corner. The third door was a dressing chamber, and she cursed the gendered arrangement of the upstairs as she bolted across the landing toward the far side of the house. As she flashed past the stairs, there was a shout from below and she growled angrily and ran faster.

She battered the door ahead with a force bolt and it catapulted into the area beyond. It was another bedroom, twice the size of the last, and painted in shades of dark-blue and brown with an enormous bed in the center. An open door on the left caught her eye, and she passed through it to discover a trophy room celebrating illegal activities. Glass cases with newspapers, books, clothes on mannequins, and old-time collector items of all kinds were on display, with small plaques explaining each. Her jaw dropped at the sight, so completely unlike anything she'd ever seen or imagined, before she shook her head with a jolt. *Get moving, Caliste.*

The rear wall held a giant gun safe, taller than she was and heavy enough that she assumed they'd had to bring it in with a crane and rebuild the wall after. *I certainly can't unlock it.* The large combination wheel had a hundred tiny numbers on it. *Damn it. Think.* Frustrated and very conscious that time was of the essence, she tapped on her sticks as she looked around for a solution. A flash of insight rocketed through her brain. She drew the weapons and told them to turn into bracelets. When they assumed liquid form to flow over her hands, she willed them to stop.

With her fingers pressed along the tiny crack between the safe door and the frame, she marshaled her intent and sent it to the magical weapon, which pushed into the gap and expanded at her urging. She poured more power into it and backed away slowly until finally, the metal creaked and deformed under the strength of the magic. *Holy hell, it worked.* It had bent enough in the right place to give her access, and she silently thanked whatever fool had selected one with a single bar lock rather than the three a safe this size would normally have.

She yanked the warped door open and reclaimed her sticks. There, in the middle of the safe, was the object of her search. She lifted the lid to ensure the pistols were in there and turned toward the doorway she'd entered through as two of the suited gangsters stuck their guns through it.

Her instinctive scream caused one to flinch and miss. The other fired and the bullet burned its way into her flesh and embedded itself in her shoulder. She'd experienced pain before, but this was nastier than anything she could remember. The shock made her stumble as she bolted for the room's other door, blasted it off its hinges, and leapt over the banister that separated the second floor from the first.

Cali focused hard on maintaining her illusion and to lock that intent into a corner of her mind to avoid giving their game away. She used a force burst from her good hand to guide her path and landed awkwardly to trip when she reached the stairs. Her newly injured arm thankfully managed to hold onto the railing.

At the bottom, two guards were as surprised to see her as she was to see them. She hurled them aside with another force blast but felt distinctly woozy from the pain—and, she realized, the loss of the blood that poured down her arm. One more full-strength force attack shredded the building's front doors, and she sprinted to where she'd last seen Tanyith. Magic streaked past her toward her pursuers. As soon as she was out of the light, a portal appeared before her with the tavern basement on the other side. She leapt through and her partner followed a moment later and closed it behind them.

Fyre sat primly on a crate. She smiled to see he was safe and heard him say, "It took you long enough," before her knees gave out and her eyes rolled back in her head.

CHAPTER THIRTY-TWO

"Easy now, there you go." Cali heard Zeb's words and felt the trickle of liquid between her lips. It was wonderfully delicious and she drank greedily as he poured the healing potion into her. It raced through her body and collected in her shoulder to cause new pain and draw a moan as it pushed the bullet out and healed the flesh behind it. When it was over, she was whole. Panting, bloody, and exhausted, but whole.

The first potion had tasted of honey and cinnamon. The next one he put to her lips was ferocious mint, and with it came a blast of magical energy that had her up on her feet in an instant. He stopped her after a few sips with a shake of his head. "If you take too much, you'll crash sooner. This counteracts the drain on your systems from the healing but eventually, that bill will come due, knocking you out whether you like it or not." He gestured toward the untouched potions in her belt. "Use them with caution if you plan to be functional tomorrow."

She pointed at the Draksa. "You still suck. But thanks for keeping them busy."

He lowered his snout in acknowledgment and his scales glistened as his tail swiped from left to right. Tanyith said, "So, no emergency rope, huh?"

Cali thought about lying but decided there was no point. "I kind of forgot and was…uh, swept up in the moment."

"Let's stick together on the next one, shall we?"

"Yeah." She nodded. "I need you to step in front of those bullets for me. That bloody hurt."

"The important part is that you succeeded, and you made it back safely," Zeb interjected. "Now, leave the case here and get the second half done. I'll keep it safe, don't you worry."

"Okay. Let's switch up our looks, shall we?" She concentrated again on the other two pictures Barton had shared. Her magic slid over Tanyith and he grew paler, his hair lightened to a beach blonde, and his beard vanished. His clothes became an ill-fitting suit. She transformed herself into another man in a bad suit who was shorter than her partner, with a buzz cut and a pale scar on his cheek. Zeb and Tanyith both nodded in approval.

Fyre barked and drew attention to the fact that he was now some kind of labrador. She grinned and said, "You know, I've always wanted a cat."

"No." His opinion on that idea was clear in the frosty growl.

"River otter?" He raised his chin and ignored her and she laughed. "Okay, then. Let's hit it, Tanyith."

He retrieved a bag next to him on a crate she hadn't

noticed before and opened the portal, and they stepped through together.

Unlike the mansion, The Shark Nightclub was dark except for a light over the front door. They crept down carefully from a rooftop across the street. As she was about to dash toward the building, Tanyith grabbed her arm. "Let's try something first." He took them a half-block away, where a large garage door and a smaller person-door nestled side by side. He used the lock tool again, and they entered without seeing any obvious indication that they'd been detected.

The interior was empty, save for a dark luxury sedan. She watched her partner, who frowned as he prowled the space. He muttered, "Okay, they could have portaled from here, but if you're going to portal anyway, why so close? It doesn't make sense." Finally, he seemed to notice something and pushed against one of the concrete blocks in the wall closest to the club. He scrambled aside as the floor beneath him—which had previously looked seamless—revealed a rectangle that descended and transformed into stairs.

He grinned. "Now we're talking. I knew it had to be there." He scrabbled in the bag, withdrew two pistols, and handed one to her. She tilted her head in a question. "They'll expect members of the Zatora gang to have guns. So, we fire them dry, manage not to hit anything, and drop them. Zeb added some magic to avoid fingerprints."

She nodded. "You had me worried there for a second."

"Remember, I was in the decent version of the group. Like, Robin Hood and the Merry Atlanteans."

Cali laughed. "Awesome. Now I picture you in tights. It's not a good look, by the way." Fyre snorted in agreement and banged against her legs. "I think someone wants to get moving."

"Yeah, me too. Sooner begun, sooner finished."

"And sooner to sleep." The effects of the energy potion were wearing off but given Zeb's warning, she wasn't ready to take more.

He led them along the passage under the street. *The magicals in New Orleans should get together and open a construction business. They'd make millions creating and maintaining basements.* It ended in a heavy steel door with no handle and a security camera. He waved into the lens, then shot it with the pistol. "Stand back." He threw a fireball and a force sphere one after the other at the door jamb and the barrier separated from it. "It looks more like an explosive device that way." He answered the question before she asked it.

They pulled the door wide and stepped inside. Tanyith destroyed another security camera, and they heard footsteps coming from the side of the room, where a staircase led upward. She positioned herself where they could see her in response to Fyre's move to stand next to the stairs. The Draksa flicked his tail out and swiped the legs out from under the first men to descend.

She fired wildly at the ones who remained upright, and when the gun clicked empty, threw it at the Atlanteans. There were five in total, two of them already on the ground. She yanked her sticks from their sheaths and willed them to be normal brown wood as she attacked the one closest. Her partner disabled the one on his side with a strike from the hilt of his sai, and Fyre tumbled the fallen thugs again as they tried to rise. The final enemy still on his feet dispatched a blast of ice at her, and she ducked and rolled away from it. *I have to remember not to use magic where they can see it.*

Her partner made short work of the scumbag who'd attacked her and together, they finished the two remaining on the floor. She yanked their belts from their trousers and used them to bind their hands and feet. "Okay, so that's the security squad. Do you think there will be more?"

Tanyith nodded. "They wouldn't want to spread the alarm if they thought they could handle it to avoid losing face in front of the others. We should still have the element of surprise. Let's get upstairs." The Draksa snaked up ahead of them, leading the way. They followed with more speed than caution. She recognized the end of the hallway they'd been down before and found the door. The man kicked it in without preamble and they discovered three people waiting inside. Usha the enemy leader looked casual in jeans and a pretty blouse with her red braids piled on her head. Her female subordinate Danna Cudon seemed as perfect as ever in her suit with a dark shirt and tie. A hulking bald man in gang street clothes had already blurred into motion.

The brute swung a punch at Cali as she ran forward, and she redirected it past her, kicked his shin to compromise his balance, and continued her approach toward the boss. *The Empress, my challenge.* She caught golden fur out of the corner of her eye as Fyre became visible. The large dog bit and pulled at the leg of the woman in the suit. A shout of pain bellowed behind her, but whether from Tanyith or the big man she couldn't be sure.

Usha raised her hand and a blast of concentrated air lashed at Cali, halting her momentum. She spun away from the focused barrage and drew and hurled her right stick in a single motion. The woman batted it away with another air spell, accompanied by a whooshing sound. She tried again with the left stick, and it met the same result. Barely in time, she dove to the side to avoid the woman's next magical attack, a thin line of force that sliced through the air like a blade.

Fyre hurtled past her unexpectedly, his airborne trajectory clearly against his will as his limbs thrashed. She instinctively threw a buffer of air ahead of him to cushion his impact against the far wall, then growled at the fact that they were not only losing, they were taking too damn long to do it. *Okay, time to play dirty.* She yelled, "Get the witch in the suit," and charged forward to launch a two-handed punch at the back of the big man's head. Her momentum channeled through her fists drove him forward into the wall as Tanyith ducked out of the way.

Her partner continued toward the woman and spun the weapons in his hands. She sneered at him and summoned a weapon of her own, a long spear of ice that trailed vapor as she swiped it through a complex pattern. She didn't hesitate but stabbed it at him as soon as he was in range. He caught it on his sai and thrust the other one at her face but Cali lost track of their battle when the desk that separated her from the boss hurtled toward her.

She rolled to the side, sure that a follow-up attack was

imminent. A force blast battered the wall beside her, so fast that she couldn't have reacted to it. She owed her continued existence to Fyre, who had shoved the enemy leader off balance. He darted away as Cali went on the offensive. She called her sticks to her hands and attacked. The woman threw a force burst at her face and she instinctively blocked it by raising the weapons in an X. The magic struck them and dissipated.

Oh, hell yes. Now we're talking. She grinned and saw doubt in the other woman's eyes. *She can't believe what she sees, which means my illusions are still holding.* She waded in with rapid strikes, and her opponent deflected them with her own small shields but backpedaled as she did so.

Instinctively, she pursued and only realized she'd been played when the Draksa crashed into her from behind and thrust her out of the path of the spear that would have taken her head off. She twisted to find her enemies and saw them fleeing. "Damn. Reinforcements will be here soon. Let's block the door again." They shoved furniture up against it, and Fyre stood ready to bolster it with an ice blast as a last resort. "Where should we look?"

Tanyith shrugged, already on the move toward a cabinet on the far side of the room. "I have no idea. Open everything." By the time they found something that looked valuable, the desk was in pieces, all the art was down from the walls, and they'd broken several statues. The object was hidden in one of the pedestals, which they only discovered by luck while shattering the sculptures atop them. She eased the long shard of metal from inside its wooden concealment and immediately noticed the symbols engraved along it. Clearly, it had been part of a larger piece, and by the sharp edges on all sides, she imagined it was from a sword. Tanyith helped her wrap it in a section of fabric cut from a drape before they stepped into a portal without delay and closed it behind them.

Cali dropped to the floor and began to laugh, and the others joined in. When she could breathe again, she pointed a finger at Tanyith. "What the hell, man? How did she get to throw a spear at me? What were you doing, dancing?"

He had the decency to look embarrassed. "She made a wicked head strike that I blocked, then flipped the weapon to cut at my feet with the other end. It turns out both sides are sharp. I had to scramble away, and that's when she did it."

"Uh-huh. Fortunately, the real hero of the day was there to save me." She smoothed her hands along the Draksa's scales, and he suddenly rolled over to allow her to rub his belly. Of course, that simply made her collapse into hysterics again.

CHAPTER THIRTY-THREE

Cali had spent the entire Friday evening shift waiting for the other shoe to drop and for one or both gangs to invade the Drunken Dragons Tavern and take her away. She'd portaled rather than walked to work in an abundance of caution and had placed magical wards on her room at the boarding house for the first time the night before.

When a tipsy witch dropped a glass to shatter on the floor with a loud crack, she almost jumped out of her skin. Zeb apparently noticed her reaction because he called her over to the bar a moment later.

He mimed patting her like one would a horse. "Calm down, girl."

The dwarf was the only person allowed to call her "girl" without receiving a punch in return like Emalia was the only one permitted to call her "child." "It's easy for you to say. You have the safest part of this whole plan."

"It was your plan."

"That is not relevant. Shut up." She grinned. "I think that somehow, you're behind it all. Mind control maybe."

"Only the fermented kind."

The door opened to admit Tanyith, which meant it was midnight or thereabouts. Zeb nodded at her, and she shouted, "Okay, people, time to clear out. We're closing early tonight." There were grumbles from the customers but nothing serious. They'd been warned as they arrived, and the proprietor had offered a discount on a final drink when he'd announced the last call a half-hour before. No one had cause for complaint except her, and then only if they tipped less because of it.

Always me getting the short end of the stick. She laughed at her own joke, knowing full well she was far luckier than she deserved with guardians, friends, magical weapons, additional training, and of course, Fyre. The illusory boxer stuck his head up from behind the bar and barked to encourage the patrons to depart faster.

By twelve-fifteen, it was empty and she and Tanyith had been banished to the building's attic. There was no ladder to access the space, so it had required a chair and a boost to get her up there, and she'd had to pull his heavy form up. The Draksa had flown around the room once to gain speed, then elevated and rocketed through the entrance with no problem. Once in place, they discovered small cracks and crevices that would permit them to watch and listen to the goings-on below.

No sooner had Zeb slid the chair away from beneath the innocuous ceiling panel than his guests began to arrive. He hadn't been willing to explain anything more about them, and she was shocked to see representatives from most of the magicals in the city come through the door. Dark and Light Elves, a wizard and a witch, a gnome, and even a Kilomea. Their host pulled a cup of his special cask brew for each, and they waited at the bar as the clock ticked the minutes off, discussing everything but the matter at hand.

At ten to one, Zeb vanished to the basement and returned with the items they'd stolen. The wizard, clearly the eldest among them, set the open case containing the pistols and the broken blade on the midpoint of the center table, cast a spell over them, and shrouded them in force. Each of the other magicals added a layer of protection—ice, shadow, fire, a mist she couldn't identify, and finally, another of force. The objects were still visible under the roiling magics but the statement was obvious—anyone dishonorable wouldn't get their hands on the items without first contending with the combined might of the group. They took up positions throughout the common room.

At one on the dot, the dwarf opened the door to admit the leadership of the Atlantean gang. The big bald man entered ahead of the others and looked irritated but unharmed. His tight white t-shirt emphasized his muscles, and his deliberate stride was a threat all on its own. Cali made a sound of disbelief, knowing she'd planted his face into the wall, and Tanyith kicked her leg from his prone position beside her. He whispered, "Scumbags can also use healing potions."

Her lips twisted in disgust, and she whispered in response, "They shouldn't be allowed to."

Next to arrive was the androgynous Danna Cudon in

her dark suit, similarly looking none the worse for wear. Her straight black hair fell over half her face, and her single visible eye scanned the room warily. Fyre puffed a small snort of cold mist into the air, apparently still irritated by the way she'd thrown him at a wall. Finally, the boss herself appeared. Usha wore a formal dark business suit with her braids bound into a long ponytail. Her flat expression concealed any emotions she might have felt.

They didn't speak and merely crossed to the far side of the bar and faced the assemblage. The humans arrived shortly after. Rion Grisham, predictably, wore an expensive suit and a red tie, while the two men accompanying him were dressed in less pricey but well-fitting business wear. Slight bulges suggested the presence of pistols in shoulder holsters. They took position on the opposite side of the room from the others near the door. Zeb moved to his usual place behind the bar facing the common room.

The old wizard stepped forward. "Thank you for coming, Mr Grisham and Ms Usha." Apparently, the man didn't know the Atlantean leader's last name either. "This may very well turn out to be a historic occasion, as the Atlanteans and the Zatora organizations meet in peace to talk." He paused as if to allow the opposing leaders an opportunity to speak, but neither did. He shrugged and continued. "So. As the representatives of various interested parties present in the Crescent City, we wish to make a request. In exchange for your agreement to our proposal, we will return the symbolic items that have come into our possession."

Usha snarled disapproval. "Thieves."

Grisham nodded with his arms folded and added, "I'm

not sure how you wound up getting my weapons from the Atlanteans, but it's certainly suspicious."

His counterpart sputtered, "Or how you acquired the shard from the Zatora hoods who stole it. I concur, suspicious."

The wizard raised an eyebrow. "Coming from you two, that's an interesting perspective. In any case, I do not know the provenance of these objects, only that they were delivered to my associate for sale and he recognized their unique importance." He nodded at the Dark Elf, who returned the gesture. "If we do not come to terms, the items will be destroyed here before your eyes. It's my understanding that this would cause you some significant...uh, public relations issues once word got out. Which it certainly would." He gestured to indicate the others around the room.

Rion Grisham's voice was mild and all the more threatening because of it. "You could all be dead by sunrise at an order from either of us." Now, it was the Atlantean who nodded over folded arms.

"You could try." The wizard shrugged again. "And the possible outcome would be that our people band together against you. How much would your 'businesses,' such as they are, suffer then? Instead, it is to everyone's benefit that you agree to our terms, which are quite reasonable."

Usha huffed out a breath and unfolded her arms. "Get to the point, old man."

Zeb interrupted. "Simple rules, so no one's confused. First, no retaliation against any of us or our people. Second, several businesses we will name are off-limits to you, including Ikehara Goro's dojo. Third, the Drunken

Dragons Tavern will be recognized neutral territory. No one will seek to claim it, and no one will cause trouble on the premises. As always, everyone will continue to be welcome here."

The opposing leaders stared at each other for almost a full minute in silence. Cali had no idea what they were doing—maybe seeking an advantage or maybe speaking telepathically. Finally, the human nodded and the Atlantean did the same.

The wizard intoned, "Give your oath, and be bound by it."

With a sigh, Grisham said, "You have my solemn oath. Neither I nor mine shall retaliate against you or your people for this affront. We will accept the names of seven businesses, one for each of you, as off-limits, and the Zatora will respect this establishment as neutral ground."

The Atlantean repeated his words with more sincerity and more anger. Tanyith leaned over and whispered, "If I had to guess, I'd say the pistols are simply symbolic, not revered. The sword piece, though, means something much deeper to her. Taking it was a violation on a different scale than the other."

"What do you think it is?"

He shook his head. "I don't know, but we'll definitely have to find out."

Below, the shields were removed and the objects returned to their owners. The humans left first and after an interval, Zeb checked to be sure they weren't lying in wait for the other faction and signaled that it was clear. The Atlanteans departed without a word, and the guests chatted amiably for several minutes before they, too, exited. He waved up at the ceiling, and they vaulted down, using magic to buffer their landings. Fyre flew another circuit of the room before he touched down near the locked door.

Cali smiled at the Draksa. "So, that went well. You have some interesting friends, Zeb."

He chuckled from his seat on one of the high chairs at the bar. "True. They're good people to have as allies."

Tanyith's voice wasn't as relieved as she would have expected. "I think allies is the right word. Because tonight, a new battle line was drawn." The dwarf nodded.

She ventured, "Everyone versus the gangs?"

Another nod from her boss confirmed her fear. "Yeah. Even though both gangs will honor their pledge, they haven't promised to accept any future actions from us without a response. They'll watch for an opportunity to strike back within the rules."

"We should have come up with some more restrictive ones."

Zeb laughed. "Did you see their faces? We were lucky to get what we got." He shook his head. "We all made some enemies tonight but it had to happen. They weren't going to stop."

"Are you sure they'll live up to their promises?"

He nodded. "I can't imagine they would want to add all of us to the gang that opposes them, so that should keep them each in check."

Tanyith's words held the doubt she felt. "Let's hope so." *Yeah. Hope for the best, but I'd better start preparing for the worst.*

CHAPTER THIRTY-FOUR

The common room was mostly empty the next afternoon when Cali stopped in for lunch. Saturdays usually didn't get busy until four or so, and she always enjoyed being there as a customer instead of a worker. The stew was a new recipe—andouille sausage, vegetables, and thick noodles in a dark gravy. It was delicious, and she was already on her second helping. Fyre, seated on the bench beside her, was finishing his third. It was entirely strange to watch him use magic to float pieces of food to his mouth, then lick the bowl clean with his long tongue.

She easily maintained the veil that kept her dining companion hidden from everyone other than Zeb or Tanyith. There was no sign of the pendulum Emalia had mentioned swinging back, so she had begun to believe her current magical strength really might be permanent. It wouldn't stop her from finding other options when she could, though. "Well rounded is well prepared," like both her Mother and Father used to say. The familiar ache of their absence resurfaced.

Tanyith took a seat across from her with his own bowl and mug in hand. His hair was again in its usual pompadour, and his beard was carefully groomed. "I have never slept better than I did last night."

She nodded. "Getting that task off our backs was a relief, especially after they agreed not to retaliate for it. Even more so since there's no way the ones we faced would have failed to report our use of magic in the Shark. My sleep was mostly untroubled, except big, green, and scaly here snores." The Draksa gave her a withering glare and went back to eating. Tanyith laughed and she pointed a spoon at him. "Don't encourage him." She shook her head. "So, what will you do now?"

He shrugged. "I guess I need to get a job since my former 'company' is no longer a viable option."

"You can come busk with me." The image of the other man performing for tips brought a grin. "You'd be a natural." *Not. But you would be hilarious.*

The door opened, and she flicked her gaze in that direction. The sight of Detective Kendra Barton elicited a groan. The woman exchanged words with Zeb before she strode across to sit beside Tanyith and across from the invisible Draksa. Cali pushed more energy into the veil.

The new arrival gave her a grin that didn't reach her eyes. They weren't accusatory but they weren't trusting either. "Cali."

"Kendra."

"He's still too old for you."

It was Cali's turn to grin. "You sound like someone with an agenda, Detective. He's not too old for you."

The other woman shook her head. "I stopped by to

check and make sure you were okay after whatever it was you were doing that you didn't want me to know you were doing."

"Fine, thanks. It turns out the whole thing was a big misunderstanding. A short talk and it was all over. Easy Peasy."

Her lips stretched in a thin smile. "That's not what I hear from the people I know. They say things have changed on the streets and that both the big gangs have pulled back to their own territories over the last day."

Tanyith matched her expression. "They gotta rest sometime. Maybe they're getting ready to try out some new strategies. They probably won't go legit, though."

"Kind of like you, huh?"

He twisted to face her. "You seem to have a problem believing I'm not part of the gang. What's your deal?"

The detective shrugged. "I've seen too many people supposedly get out, only to be right back in line the moment things got tough."

"Trust me, lady, things would be way tougher for me in than they are out."

"So you say."

He shook his head, clearly exasperated. Cali interrupted. "So, you've checked in. It was lovely to see you. You can go now."

"One more thing." Barton chuckled. "You did me a solid, and you were right. Those four were ready to leave town once they discovered they'd attacked the other gang without orders and gave us information in exchange for transport. There is a group of Atlanteans coming in on a cruise ship next week." She tossed a card on the table with the normally blank side upward showing a name and date written on it.

The woman gave them a dismissive wave as she walked back to the bar, shared a word and a laugh with Zeb, and aimed toward the door. Before she left, she turned and stared hard at Cali with her blank detective face. "I'll have my eyes on you both."

She called, "Not if we see you first," but the woman was already out of the tavern.

Tanyith laughed. "Mature."

"I don't need to be mature. You're the old one. Well, you and Zeb."

The dwarf joined them at the table with three cups in his hands. Each was half full, and she recognized his cask special inside. "It's the last of the batch so it's fitting that we share it." He raised his cup. "To the three of you. Because of your actions, New Orleans is a little more just than it was a week ago."

They clinked the glasses together and drank half of it. The liquid burned its way down into her stomach. It was cleansing, leaving a purity in its wake. She smiled at her friends, feeling freer than she had since the discovery of her parents' secret restraint of her magic. Despite the drama of the notion, she knew in her soul a connection existed between the city's need for champions and the revelation of her power. Perhaps Tanyith's return was part of fulfilling that same need. In any case, this moment felt more like a beginning than an ending.

She raised her own glass. "To all those who are willing to stand for what's right." They touched glasses in silence and finished their drinks.

Zeb collected the empty glassware and frowned at her with mirth in his eyes. "All right, hop down off your fancy pedestal and get to work. Break time's over. I'm not paying you to sit around."

Her scathing reply never reached her lips. The Draksa dispelled his veil and snorted icy mist over her, which made her yelp and fall off the bench in an attempt to avoid it. By the time she got back up, the others were laughing so hard they wouldn't listen. She glared at Fyre, who gave her a completely innocent look. "Oh, you'll pay for that, lizard breath. When you least expect it."

His fake scared look made them laugh more. Cali gave up and headed to the bar to prep for the dinner crowd. *You'll all pay. Wait and see.*

CHAPTER THIRTY-FIVE

Rion Grisham sat on the new couches that decorated his basement office. After the violation of the space by the Atlanteans several nights before, he'd had it ripped down to the frame, then fixed and redecorated. The teams had worked around the clock and overall, it was an improvement.

On the couch arranged at a ninety-degree angle to his own were the two men who had accompanied him to the dwarf's tavern. The one on the left was his second in command and clearly attempted to model himself after his boss—same clothes, same hair, and same shaven face. The one on the right was a highly paid wizard who had a personal grudge against the Atlanteans and had thus been willing to ally with the gang. He wore jeans and a sweat-shirt, and there was no way to be certain that the face he saw was the mage's real one. The disguise he'd worn at the meeting had been an entirely different person.

Grisham asked, "What are your recommendations?"

His lieutenant responded instantly. "Hit the streets

harder. We've been gentler than we need to. Let's put the screws to anyone who resists. If we move quickly, we can expand our territory so fast the Lants won't be able to stop us. Then, we'll have more resources to squash them like the bugs that they are."

The wizard had begun to shake his head from the first words. "That's not enough. Yes, let's do that. But we need to strike directly at those who oppose us now. We can't wait until the situation improves. We must do both immediately. And not only the Atlanteans. Everyone."

The first man countered, "That adds considerable risk. We were here before them and can outlast them."

"No. You don't understand. Right now, you picture a two-sided battle with spectators. But it's not that at all. We have more than one set of enemies—the other gang and the allegedly neutral dwarf and his friends. They've joined the game and present a danger to us. You don't really buy that the items somehow happened to come to the Dark Elf, I'm sure."

Grisham nodded thoughtfully. "Those are both valid points. But there's one more thing. You need to track down the ones who were in here. You saw them on the security footage. We need to make a public example of them or no one will believe us when we threaten them." He leaned forward and stared from one to the other. "Do it. Do it all. Locate them, put pressure on the streets, and find a way to strike at the dwarf and his people. I want results, and I want them now."

He leaned back as they filed from the room. *Blood is the only thing that will cleanse the stain on this house.*

Across town, at the bar of the otherwise empty Shark Nightclub, Usha and Danna sat with short glasses of heavily spiced rum in front of them. She drained hers in one drink and set it down hard. Her subordinate did the same, then asked, "Ready?"

She nodded. "As ready as anyone can be for this experience. Remember, you are present but silent. She will not take kindly to any interruption."

"Got it." Danna stood and straightened the bright blue tie she wore over her black shirt. "Quiet as a mouse."

"Quieter." The boss smoothed her dress, which was covered in a colorful pattern that resembled light shining through blue waves. With a deep breath, she strode deliberately through the back door. She turned into the room the Zatora intruders had wrecked and shook her head at the damage. It had been left in disarray to remind herself of what was at stake. She crossed to the right-hand wall and whispered a spell to reveal a hidden door. The large pearl ring on her finger fit perfectly into a small hole, and she rotated her wrist.

The door unlocked with a click and swung outward. Inside was a cramped room, barely the size of a walk-in closet. They crowded in and the door closed, leaving them in darkness. The sound of waves filled the space as a glow appeared in the front of the room and the increased illumination revealed a sphere in the center of a basin of water that rested on a stone pedestal. A mist slowly gathered above it and undulated in place.

After several minutes, the vapors suddenly coalesced

into a face. It was clearly female, with high cheekbones, sculptured eyebrows, and piercing eyes. Her hair was made of thick tentacles that waved softly in the air as if it was water, and the hint of a thick necklace was present where the image ended in the middle of her throat. She sounded irritated and a palpable sense of dread filled the small chamber. "Yes? What do you have to report?"

Usha locked her spine and raised her chin. "Our plans proceed apace, Your Highness. However, new players have entered the field."

"And this matters why?"

"A former member of this group, Tanyith, is among them."

The image laughed. "Ah, there is a name from the past. I presume he is as troublesome now as he was then?"

She raised an eyebrow in surprise as she'd expected anger, not amusement. "Indeed so."

The woman shrugged. "Then eliminate him. Eliminate them all. We must control this city if our plans are to succeed. You are the linchpin. Do you require assistance?"

Pride warred with practicality, and the latter won. She bowed her head. "Yes. A couple of enforcers would be helpful."

"You shall have them within the day. But fail me, and they will be your doom."

"Understood."

"Do you have anything more?"

"No, Your Highness. Thank you."

The image vanished without a response. Her subordinate exhaled noisily as the door swung open again and stepped quickly from the room. Usha followed and laughed inwardly at the effect of the audience on the other woman. *It was much the same for me, once.* "Are you well?"

Danna sank to the floor and worked visibly to control her trembling. "She is...uh, overwhelming."

"Yes. That is only one of the reasons she is our empress. And we cannot—must not—fail her. There are indeed fates worse than death, and unless we claim this city for New Atlantis, we will experience all of them."

The adventures don't end here. Join Cali, Zeb and their band of magical outsiders as they try to keep New Orleans safe in Mystical Alley Groove!

If you enjoyed this book, you may also enjoy the first series from T.R. Cameron, also set in the Oriceran Universe. The Federal Agents of Magic series begins with Magic Ops and it's available now at Amazon and through Kindle Unlimited.

FBI Agent Diana Sheen is an agent with a secret...

...She carries a badge and a troll, along with a little magic.

But her Most Wanted List is going to take a little extra effort.

She'll have to embrace her powers and up her game to take down new threats,

Not to mention deal with the troll that's adopted her.

All signs point to a serious threat lurking just beyond sight, pulling the strings to put the forces of good in harm's way.

Magic or mundane, you break the law, and Diana's gonna find you, tag you and bring you in. Watch out magical baddies, this agent can level the playing field.

It's all in a day's work for the newest Federal Agent of Magic.

AUTHOR NOTES - TR CAMERON

OCTOBER 15, 2019

Thank you for reading the first book in the *Scions of Magic* series! I hope you loved it as much as I loved writing it. I am grateful every day for the continued opportunity to connect with you through the stories we share.

This novel was written at home, at my gym, in airports, on planes, at a conference in Florida, on the bus, in the hospital (not as a patient fortunately), and in Panera. It's been a busy time, but the characters and story have made me eager to return to the page every day and provided a refuge from the stresses around me. I hope they've done the same for you!

This tiny corner of the Oriceran Universe is a collaboration between me, Martha Carr, and Michael Anderle (who have written a ton of other works in the Oriceran timelines). It was just under a year ago that I wrote a short story for the Oriceran "Fans Write" anthology to try to convince Michael and Martha I had the chops to write in the fantastic world they'd created. Nine novels later, it's going smashingly well (from my perspective, anyway.

Their author notes are after mine, so perhaps there's a conflicting view in there somewhere). I come up with a half-formed idea, and they bring their giant brains to bear and make it a trillion or so times better. I am exceedingly lucky to have such amazing people to work with.

I came to this one with the idea of a Dwarf owning a bar, a desire to flesh out the Atlanteans who were a really cool feature of the Leira Chronicles series, and a main character who was just starting to grow into her powers. Several elements of the plot and characters came from my collaborators, including the trope-breaking pacifist Dwarf, the prison break from Trevilsom, and some other fun stuff that will appear in future books.

New Orleans is my second favorite city in the United States, right after my hometown of Pittsburgh, so to write in that setting is truly a pleasure. It's also the perfect melting pot for the Atlantean subculture to blend in and work their plans to establish a foothold on the continent from which to expand.

I'm an avid gamer in my occasional spare time, and I'm playing *Control* at the moment, and waiting for *Outer Worlds*. I'm totally a sucker for story-based computer RPGs, and that one has some real promise. And I'm counting the days to season four of the *Expanse*. Plus, since I'm a *Star Wars* fan, December is going to be a big month, and as a *Star Trek* fan, January will be just as big!

My eight-year-old daughter wants to write books with me, so that's our current background project: figuring out where our interests meet to do it. She's all about Minecraft and Spider-Man at the moment, and doesn't understand licensing issues yet, so negotiations continue.

If you're looking for another new read until book 2 comes out and haven't checked out my other series, you totally should! There's the Federal Agents of Magic, also set in the Oriceran Universe, and the Chaos Shift Cycle, a military sci-fi space opera set in its own universe. They share a focus on action, sharp banter, and imperfect heroes taking on powerful enemies. Plus, of course, there's the incredible library of collected works from Martha Carr and Michael Anderle!

Until next time, joys upon joys to you and yours – so may it be.

PS: If you'd like to chat with me, here's the place. I check in daily or more: https://www.facebook.com/AuthorTRCameron. For more info on my books, and to join my reader's group, please visit www.trcameron.com.

AUTHOR NOTES - MARTHA CARR

OCTOBER 25, 2019

It was a lively week in New York City hanging out with my godchild, Janine. We were there for my friend David's birthday and we came a little early to do some shopping and take in the 911 memorial, maybe walk through Central Park.

The day of the guided tour for the memorial was as clear and blue as the day it happened over 18 years ago. If you go, take the guided walking tour because there is so much to find out about how carefully they laid out the trees and how the names are arranged on the memorials, and more. It adds something even deeper and richer when you walk into the museum, which by the way is so much bigger than it looks from the outside.

Here and there, tucked into an occasional name was a white rose placed there by a volunteer to signify that person's birthday.

Over thirty-five years ago when I was in my early 20's and living in New York City I used to travel through the Twin Towers (the North building I think) picking up a few groceries as I caught the subway. There were a lot of stores inside the very big building. One of those times I stopped in a small grocery store and went up to the counter and held up the last bit of money I had for a month.

"I have eight dollars. What will that buy me?" I asked.

The older store owner who looked like someone's dad picked up a full-size brown paper bag and wrote $8.00 on the outside and handed it to me, saying, "Fill it."

"With anything?" I asked, doing my best not to cry. I hated crying in public, but it was tough. He nodded his head and repeated himself. "Fill it up." I've never forgotten his kindness and as I looked over the edge at the memorial I wondered where his shop had once stood and hoped he had long since retired.

The museum is deep and winds around and around with a carefully curated display that starts with the 1993 bombing and moves to just before the planes hit and includes the Pentagon and the crash in rural Pennsylvania. All of the lighting is lowered giving a solemn air and everyone moves through the different displays quietly and respectfully. One small room is on a continuous loop announcing the name of someone who died, a brief memory and their photo. Another room shows things donated by the families and plays a voicemail from someone on an upper level of the North Tower, which means he didn't survive. A destroyed fire truck and the cement stairs from inside the building that were used by some to successfully escape were in there. Some of the items stretch for two stories and some are small enough to hold in the palm of your hand. There's so much and it's apparent that so much thought and care went into everything.

By the time we emerged into the sunlight we were exhausted and had walked over ten thousand steps. It all seemed a little surreal and spoke to the courage, resilience and in the end, the hope of the American people. As someone said in one of the recorded voices, "Hold your grief gently." And then we get up and rebuild and go forward and believe in the possibilities again, changed by our experience. More adventures to follow.

OTHER SERIES IN THE ORICERAN UNIVERSE:

THE DANIEL CODEX SERIES

I FEAR NO EVIL

THE UNBELIEVABLE MR. BROWNSTONE

ALISON BROWNSTONE

SCHOOL OF NECESSARY MAGIC

SCHOOL OF NECESSARY MAGIC: RAINE CAMPBELL

FEDERAL AGENTS OF MAGIC

SCIONS OF MAGIC

THE LEIRA CHRONICLES

REWRITING JUSTICE

THE KACY CHRONICLES

MIDWEST MAGIC CHRONICLES

SOUL STONE MAGE

THE FAIRHAVEN CHRONICLES

OTHER BOOKS BY JUDITH BERENS

BOOKS BY MICHAEL ANDERLE

For a complete list of books by Michael Anderle, please visit

www.lmbpn.com/ma-books/

All LMBPN Audiobooks are Available at Audible.com and iTunes. For a complete list of audiobooks visit:

www.lmbpn.com/audible

CONNECT WITH MICHAEL ANDERLE

Michael Anderle Social

Website:

http://www.lmbpn.com

Email List:

http://lmbpn.com/email/

Facebook Here:

https://www.facebook.com/OriceranUniverse/

https://www.facebook.com/TheKurtherianGambitBooks/

Made in the USA
Columbia, SC
11 April 2020

91647592R00176